A BETTER CLASS
OF PEOPLE

A BETTER CLASS OF PEOPLE

— *a novel in stories* —

Robert Lopez

DZANC
BOOKS

DZANC
BOOKS

5220 Dexter Ann Arbor Rd.
Ann Arbor, MI 48103
www.dzancbooks.org

Library of Congress Cataloging-in-Publication Data Available Upon Request

ISBN: 978-1-950539-42-0
First US edition: March 2022
Interior design by Michelle Dotter
Jacket design by Steven Seighman

Printed in the United States of America

10 9 8 7 6 5 4 3 2 1

Contents

For Jenny

Furloughs,
or How to Stand in Traffic

Come morning I stand in traffic. I set my alarm for daybreak and get out of bed when it goes off. Other people stay in bed after the alarm goes off, but I don't understand people like this and these days I don't bother trying. Maybe years ago I tried to understand these people. I asked questions and tried listening to the answers but after a while I stopped all that. Back then I would stay in bed, too, like they did, and then I'd go to work like they would, via the train or highway, but then I stopped all that, too.

Now when the alarm goes off I know it's time to go stand in traffic and so that's what I do, when I can, when I'm allowed out of the house.

I haven't told anyone I stand in traffic. So far no one's asked what I do in the morning, and I'm not one to volunteer information. If they ask I'll tell them it's to stretch my legs or get some air.

No one can argue with someone wanting to stretch legs or get air.

I love the outdoors, regardless of weather. I love seeing the sky above me and how blue or gray it is depending on if it's blue or gray. I love breathing in cool, crisp air, whether it is filled with exhaust fumes or not. For me being outside is glorious. It's like food.

I can't remember what I did for work but it wasn't outside in the weather, under the crisp air and sky. They had me in a building inside a room and cubicle all day and would only let me go come the end of it.

I never stand in the same intersection twice in a row, which is something I won't tell them if they ask. I don't need anyone figuring out what intersection I'm about to go stand in before I have a chance to stand there myself.

I also mix up parts of town.

I used to wake in the morning and go to work and it didn't matter where the work was or if I had to take a train or bus or even drive myself to get there, I'd do it every single day until I realized who cared anymore. This is when I told them I won't be coming back and they said what's the difference.

So now I stand in traffic in the morning but never at night. I only tried to do it once at night and I didn't like it.

I catalog what happens during the day. I go through notebook after notebook and it helps me stay organized.

When I say it helps I mean I try to keep track of everything. What people say, what they do, where they sit and stand and how they talk out loud in front of everybody.

I haven't been able to sort anything out yet or come to any conclusions.

Last week I asked them for a new notebook during the noontime meeting because the old one was filled with inscrutable data.

We tell stories about our lives and try to listen to each other without our heads exploding.

I have been here for as long as I can remember, which is probably between two weeks and twelve years. I'm not sure if I brought myself here or someone did it for me. I do know that it was a good idea, that it wasn't going well for me inside that cubicle.

I try not to think about this when I am out in traffic. When you are out in traffic, you cannot think about what happened earlier that day, you cannot think about what happened last night, you cannot think about what happened to you years ago when you had a family and colleagues. You have to breathe in through your nose and out through your mouth and not think of anything at all.

I keep track of who fidgets and squirms and touches what during our meetings but it's hard because I can't remember anyone's name. I refer to people by a distinguishing characteristic if I can find one.

Yesterday Watermelon Man asked me if I like to watch horrible movies. I figured he meant horror movies and I told him no, which is the truth. Then he asked if I liked dogs and I told him it depends. I told him dogs are better than people but that's nothing to brag about. He said that for years he had a pet dog but lost him in an accident.

I didn't ask what kind of accident, but I told him that's awful and I'm sorry. Then I told him to shut the fuck up so he could get better.

All of us are here to get better, and if I get enough sleep at night it means I can stand in traffic come morning. You can't stand in traffic if you haven't had a good night's sleep.

This is when I bring traffic to a halt, when I'm fresh and well rested, but only if I'm allowed out. You are not always allowed out here.

I call these furloughs but I don't think anyone else calls these furloughs.

Watermelon Man is called Watermelon Man because he has these marks on his fat red face that look like seeds, which go well with the size of his head, which is enormous.

When I am out on furlough I walk right out into the middle of a busy intersection and I stand there and wait for something to happen. Sometimes people don't even see me out there. Sometimes they drive by and I can feel the rush of air as they go past.

It is a glorious feeling.

You can lose your balance if you're not careful but this only happened to me once. The problem was I had no center of gravity. I think it was a station wagon that almost knocked me over from the rush of air. I stumbled into a different lane but there were no cars driving there so I didn't get run over.

You have to stand wide and crouch down when you stand in traffic. You have to get up on your toes, the balls of your feet. I don't know why they call them the balls of your feet, but even still you have to get up on them. And I'm not sure you can stand wide and crouch down at the same time. And even if you could you probably couldn't get up on the balls of your feet while doing it.

I do know you have to do some combination of these things if you want to remain upright when a station wagon speeds by at sixty miles an hour.

You cannot think of your old life when you are out in traffic. You cannot think of how you used to go to work like everyone else and you cannot think about your family that never comes to visit you.

To be fair I'm not sure my family knows I'm here.

I'm not sure anyone in my family is still alive.

You have to be certain no police officers are present when you stand in traffic.

The police will shoot anyone who stands in traffic or crosses against the lights or calls them on the phone for help.

We talk about which of us have been shot or brutalized by the police during our meetings and almost everyone has a story to tell and the scars to prove it.

Watermelon Man can't go more than thirty minutes without falling asleep or crying, but during those thirty minutes he is fascinating. I write down most of what he says and I promise not to share it because he's afraid of libel or slander or defamation.

Some motorists slam on brakes and swerve to avoid running me over. Sometimes they crash into other cars. So far no one has been injured when crashing into another car. No one has gone through a windshield like my brother did once.

I cannot remember much about my family but I can remember my brother going through the windshield. I can still see his head making contact with the glass and crashing through it. I can see his body careening off the hood and landing on the pavement.

What's funny is I was driving him to the hospital when this happened.

Some neighborhood kids beat him senseless because of a rumor they'd heard. I can't remember what was rumored or if I was the one who started it.

I was never one to cast aspersions, but I was one to start rumors.

I didn't know I had a brother for the longest time.

Right after every car skids to a stop the people get out and rush over to me. Some are frantic and concerned. They think there's something wrong with me. They think I am old and demented or young and troubled. They ask if I'm okay, if I'm hurt, if I know where I am, who I am. I tell them I think I'm okay, that I think the bleeding has stopped but I have a funny taste in my mouth and it hurts when I blink my eyes. I tell them that I am out here protesting and they ask protesting what and I answer everything. Some put their arms around me and usher me to the side of the road. They tell me they are going to call for an ambulance. They tell me I should be careful, that I should look both ways. They tell me it's a good thing a cop didn't see.

Some people call me names but I won't repeat what they say.

The slurs have to do with my ethnicity and intelligence.

It's possible Watermelon Man and I were colleagues. I think we were kept inside a cubicle in a room in a building and had to consult each other on projects and proposals.

I never share this during the noontime meeting. I also never talk about Esperanza, my puzzle and punishment.

When it comes my turn to share, I talk about my brother and what it was like growing up both before I knew he existed and after.

I think maybe life was glorious before I learned I had a brother.

You cannot be afraid when standing in traffic. You have to realize you might get run over at any time. You have to be at peace with yourself and your maker, if you have one.

I think I remember my mother sitting me down and saying there was something I should know. I asked if it was absolutely necessary, that I knew too much already. She said I had a bastard brother and that my father was his father and God knows how many others there were.

I don't think Watermelon Man is my brother because we look nothing like each other. My head is not big and my face is not red and fat with seeds all over it.

But in some ways he's the brother I never had instead of the one I did.

Sometimes I leave on my robe and slippers when I go to stand in traffic. Sometimes I steal someone's cane and it's like I have a scepter and I'm sure I look majestic. I see the faces of my subjects speeding past and it is a look of awe and wonder.

I never make a sign and hang it around my neck. Other people don't need to know what I'm protesting.

I'm out there because everything has gone too far and someone has to put a stop to it.

I don't remember what my brother was wearing when he went through the windshield, but it was the only time we were ever in a car together.

I was out of the hospital the following week, but he wound up living there for the rest of his life, mostly comatose, but always hooked up to machines that did everything for him mechanically, like breathing and eating and drinking and going to the bathroom.

Finally, they pulled the plug for him and everyone said it was about time.

Soon word will spread about what I'm doing. Soon people will stand in traffic all over the world and it will be because of me.

In this way I'll be famous like other revolutionaries. People like Martin Luther King Jr. and Gandhi and Che Guevara and Jesus.

I didn't actually see my brother go through the windshield, didn't see his body careening off the hood and landing in a heap of broken glass some thirty feet in front of the car.

The reason I didn't see all of this is because I was unconscious at the time.

But I have imagined this happening to my brother, usually in slow motion, as I'm sure it happened too fast in real life.

In my imagination he is like an acrobat sailing through the air. I picture him doing handsprings and forward rolls, although you probably can't do that while midair. Sometimes I see him landing on his feet, not even breaking stride as he walks off to a gas station to buy cigarettes.

It is important to pick out an intersection that has good visibility and sightlines. You want the drivers to see you, otherwise it is pointless.

I probably shouldn't be allowed out of the house but they allow me out. They allow most of the others out but I don't talk to any of them. I don't know what these people do when they are allowed out on furlough. I don't know if any of them go stand in traffic or where they might do it.

I don't think Watermelon Man is allowed out and this I agree with.

They are not very good at what it is they do here, which is helping people get better. They say that everyone gets better at their own pace, that we shouldn't compare ourselves to others.

I'm talking about the doctors and nurses and other government officials that work here. They all wear the same suits and ties and tell people what is wrong with them and how they should be ashamed of themselves.

Watermelon Man says they want all the agitators in one place to keep us quiet.

I don't know whom to believe.

I am allowed out once a month, usually over a weekend. I call these furloughs but they are not officially called furloughs. I know this because I thanked one of them for the furlough last month and he said what the fuck is a furlough.

I never see my brother when I'm out on furlough. He is never out on the street or in the middle of traffic.

He could be anywhere in the world or he could be dead and buried.

I didn't stick around to find out what happened to him after they pulled the plug. Most people die within minutes, but maybe for him there was a miracle.

If there's anyone I'd tell about standing in traffic it's the one who said what the fuck is a furlough.

He wears an orange jumpsuit and always has with him a mop and a bucket and a Glock 9mm. He also conducts the noontime meetings. He sits in a chair in the middle of the room and calls on people.

He asks questions and pretends to listen to the answers, brandishes his weapon, tells everyone to please settle down and stop touching yourself.

He asked me once how I was getting on. I told him I was making great progress. He said that was splendid.

I didn't tell him how I stand in traffic for five whole minutes before something happens. Before someone slams on the brakes and causes an accident or someone calls the police to chase me away.

This is because I can stand quiet. I can almost make myself invisible.

So far no one has seen me on my way out the door, which is further proof of my invisibility. But if I'm stopped I'll tell them I'm going to stretch my legs, get some air. This is the second thing you have to do before standing in traffic.

The first thing is to set the alarm for daybreak. It is the best time to stand in traffic, out there in the dim light of a new day, when people are still groggy and careless.

Never say something like to the barricades on your way out the door.

Then find a busy intersection somewhere, one with good sightlines and plenty of traffic.

Stand quiet. Stand wide.

Breathe in through your nose and out through your mouth.

Know that what you're doing will change the world, that you're a revolutionary.

Know that this is better than going to work every day and sitting inside a cubicle in an office until you're dead and they say what's the difference.

A Good Percentage

All of the women sitting across from the baby are looking at the baby. They are smiling. I cannot see what the baby is doing but whatever it's doing is making all of the women sitting across from it smile. Five of the seven women have nice smiles, which is a good percentage. The other two are smiling like they hate the baby, like they wish the baby were dead or on another subway. These two probably cannot have a baby themselves. They want one but can't have one. It is sad, but not unusual. One can't conceive and the other can't carry to term and now they hate this baby and the baby's mother as they hate all babies and all mothers. I don't judge these women. I know what it's like. I am on my way home to drink myself asleep and maybe try to make weekend plans with Esperanza, who has been avoiding me of late.

The People Who Need It

I don't know what's wrong with the television, but I'm still a person, still someone that people should know something about, should maybe feel sorry for, too. What I'm saying is I turn the television on but can't get a picture. It's the same thing with the telephone. I pick it up but can't get a dial tone. Sometimes I think I'm dead, that this is what happens to you when you die.

I can look out the window but this means nothing. I see people out there in the world but maybe they are all dead, too.

The dead people outside are dressed in layers because it is cold. Tonight they say it'll be in the single digits.

I remember I was alive once because I went outside into the freezing cold and walked to the store and bought pie and groceries and then brought those pies and groceries home and stored them in the pantry and refrigerator.

I had a job once, too.

I also used to play tennis. I would play with my friend and then one glorious day I played with his sister, whose backhand slice was devastating, whose first serve was unimaginable.

The stakes were agreed upon beforehand. Should she win, I was to leave her alone forever. Should I win, she'd have to sleep with me.

I was using her brother as leverage, as I had him bound and gagged at an undisclosed location. This is how she agreed to play.

To this day people still talk about that match.

How you know you're alive is it's freezing cold and you feel it and it's horrible. How you know you are dead is it's freezing cold and you still feel it and it's even more horrible.

I am always cold on account of my bloodline, which is half Puerto Rican and half God knows what.

I never knew where my mother's people came from because she never spoke of it and whenever I asked she would beat me with a rolling pin or ladle.

Half Ricans aren't meant to live this far north, aren't meant to live through an ice age.

I never prepared a meal for myself but I always made sure I had plenty of groceries. I never wanted to go to the pantry or open the refrigerator and find it empty.

In the pantry there was flour and sugar and salt and in the refrigerator there was butter and vegetable shortening. I'm not sure if the vegetable shortening belonged in the refrigerator but that's where I kept it.

This is what you need to make a pie crust. Maybe there's more to it but I don't think there is.

No one has ever made a pie for me because everyone I know is horrible.

I'd read pie recipes and collect books about pie and stack them up against the wall opposite the window. I wanted books from floor to ceiling.

I had other books, too, but vowed not to read them until I was finished with all the pie books.

Instead I bought pies that came in boxes already assembled and baked.

It is always freezing cold now because it is the most recent ice age and we are in the middle of it. They say this one will last for hundreds if not thousands of years.

I suppose I'm lucky that I can remember a time when it wasn't freezing cold, like the day I played tennis against my friend's sister.

Temperatures that day were in the mid-nineties and there were intermittent thunderstorms as well.

I would stack the pies up alphabetically in the pantry and I would eat pie every night for dinner. Blueberry, Strawberry, Pumpkin or Plum.

I never alphabetized the pie books.

I can't remember the last time I opened the refrigerator or pantry so I don't know if everything is still in there.

It is colder outside than it is in the refrigerator the last time I checked. But I can't remember the last time I was outside or the last time I opened the refrigerator.

I also can't remember what my job entailed or how much money I made. I think I held a prestigious position and had a great many underlings. I remember telling people what to do and they did it without question, without fail.

The screen is blank but I know it's on. I can hear it buzzing, can hear the inside machinations. There is life inside the television but there's no proof, no picture.

It might be like my own body. I can hear the heart beating and feel the blood flowing through the veins and arteries and I can sense the liver groaning and the gall bladder flailing.

It might be too cold for the television to work. It is almost as cold in my apartment as it is outside.

Years ago the television worked fine. I would scan the channels from 2 to 80 and back again for hours at a time. I'd spend five or so seconds on each station. What was on television wasn't important to me. That I was looking for something is what mattered. I was a seeker.

I am dressed in layers inside my own home, though no one can see this, not even me.

Like the television I don't have a picture. There are no pictures of me in this apartment, framed or otherwise. There are no mirrors, either.

There's no sound coming from the television, except for one time. I heard something like a game show, someone who sounded like a host talking to people who sounded like contestants.

It's possible that was the job I can't remember. I might've been a game show host. I have a vague memory of lights and cameras and horrible people acting like imbeciles.

I also might've been a professional tennis player or a telemarketer, but probably not a police officer because I am a better class of people.

There is the red light indicating the television is on, but it isn't on, not by any measure.

I think the window has been painted shut. I don't know what this means but I've heard the expression.

I'm not sure how a window could get painted shut, how the paint would keep it shut. I don't know if it is a special paint they sell.

I can see my breath, in my home, in the middle of the day.

That I can see my breath doesn't mean I'm alive.

People would ask me why I'd eat pie every night and my answer was always the same.

Now no one asks me anything. I remember once I had a particular underling who was even more horrible than the rest and she would ask me questions all the time. She would wear see-through blouses and tight-fitting skirts and open-toed shoes so you know it was hopeless.

I used to call her Ursula the Horrible but her name was Magdalene.

She would ask me how I got to be on television, how I got my start, what's it like being famous and if there's anything I could do for you.

I've never told Esperanza about Ursula because how could I.

I would sit in my chair in front of a giant mirror while they put makeup on me. I'd drink from a coffee cup filled with bourbon and spout curses at the underlings.

Nearby there would be underlings doing what I told them to do, without question, without fail.

One was in charge of keeping my coffee cup filled with bourbon and cleaning my guns. I'd send this one to the store with a list of which bourbons were acceptable and which weren't and which gun oils were acceptable and which weren't.

This one was in love with Ursula and it was obvious. I'd watch him watch her from across the room, a particular look on his face, a mixture of lust and evil intent.

I'd tell him what Ursula did to me last night. I'd make him listen to every single word and ask him what he thought at the end of every sentence.

This happened back when men and women could still carry on affairs with each other.

I told him we ate pie for dinner and I said, what do you think of that?

Then I told him we sat on either side of the table in my kitchen, the pie resting on a high hat in the middle of the table, candles flickering between us.

I said, how do you like that?

I told him we didn't even move to the bedroom after we were done, that we took turns on each other right at the table, that she used the pie filling as a massage oil, that he wouldn't believe what she did with this filling, how she used it, and how I poured the wax on her one drip at a time until the candle was down to a molten stump.

I said, how does that work on you?

Before he could answer I walked out of the dressing room.

Actually I don't think this is right, not most of it anyway. I don't think I worked as a game show host with underlings applying makeup and bourbon. I think it was a saloon, one that had swinging doors, like in the old days, like in the movies.

I have a vague memory of dim lights and sawdust and people behaving like imbeciles.

I think Ursula was an actress. She would wear see-through tops and tight skirts and open-toed shoes.

I do know the telephone has never rung in my home and I have never answered it.

The telephone might be ornamental. It might be a prop.

This memory of listening to a dial tone for two hours might be a dream or something that I saw on the television back when it was still working.

It's possible I've had both jobs at different times or it's possible I saw a movie once with a guy who looked like me and had both jobs in the movie.

The problem is I can't remember how I used to look, back when I was alive. I think I was very handsome because I remember Ursula telling me this over and over.

I think she thought I would help her with her film career. I think she was under the impression I had contacts in the film business.

I may've told her I could make her a star is the reason.

The dressing room might've been the back office and it was always cold back there, like it is now. There was a dartboard and neon signs and a wall calendar with a half-naked girl looking down on everyone.

Ursula would let me take pictures of her when she was half naked, three-quarters naked, but never fully naked. She was always respectable like that.

If I had to guess I'd say I was tall and swarthy with an excellent physique. I was probably a world-class athlete, as I have a dim memory of playing tennis in front of massive crowds all over the world.

The color and shape of my eyes were stunning, with perfect brows framing them just so. The forehead, which only bore the slightest hints of age, was in perfect proportion with a mop of curly black hair sitting atop it. Full lips with a charming birthmark edging toward the right corner and a dimpled chin obscured by a salt-and-pepper beard, neatly trimmed, with a line moving from the top of my ears in a perfect L shape to the rim of my mouth.

I'm sure there was a glow.

I'd stand behind the bar and pour drinks for the regulars. I'd watch Ursula serving the customers because she was the cocktail waitress trying to be an actress trying to be a movie star. I didn't know how to make most drinks, so I'd make a whiskey sour or a gin and tonic and tell them to drink it.

Only once or twice did I have to shoot a customer in the face.

Tonight, they say, it'll be in the single digits, which is even colder than usual. When I say they I mean the people on the radio. I have an old transistor and it still works.

They say people should beware. They say people should stay home, dress in layers. They are talking about me, I think, but they don't know that I'm already home, already dressed in layers.

Sometimes I think of myself as a contestant on a game show but I don't know the rules or what I'm supposed to do or if anyone is watching.

I'm not sure if I'm dead because I've been here for as long as I can remember and I'm not sure if I miss Ursula or wonder where she is or if she is one of the dead people outside, freezing.

If they are not actually dead they might as well be.

I feel safe because I have my gun collection hidden behind the stack of pie books.

Time goes by or it doesn't. I don't have any watches or clocks and on the radio they never tell me the time, only the weather.

This is what I do to pass the time, if there is time to pass. I look out the window and listen to the radio. I also read from the stacks of books. I am always careful when I remove a book so the others will not fall down all over me.

There is no door here, only the window that's painted shut, but I'm so high up I can't climb out of it and into the world below.

I can probably jump out the window or maybe not out the window but through it. I'd have to break through the glass.

Sometimes I think about doing this. They call it defenestration, which I learned from one of the books.

I'd want to test it first, which is why I'm going to defenestrate a book tomorrow morning.

I probably wouldn't survive the fall and would be dead once I hit the pavement.

There is a book in here I read every day. I start at the beginning and read on through till the end.

Each time it is like I'm reading it anew as I can never remember what the story is about.

It's almost like every day the book tells me a different story.

Today someone fell asleep sitting up, after watching birds and squirrels feed from a feeder. There were three different kinds of birds fluttering about and acrobatic squirrels pilfering the bird food.

No one mentioned how cold it was, but that's what I assume, that it was freezing cold. There was no mention of what anyone was wearing, but I imagine all the characters wrapped up in coats and scarves or see-through blouses and tight skirts.

There was no mention of what the character did for a living, if they were a game show host or a saloon manager or what.

The character that fell asleep had a niece named Chloe, who is almost two in the story. Chloe comes into the room, places her elbows on the ottoman where this person is resting his legs, puts her hands together and clasps, fingers interlacing with the other fingers. She closes her eyes as if she's concentrating.

The character asked his sister if Chloe prays for people and the sister said, only for people who need it.

Sometimes I think I wrote this book because I think I had a sister who had a daughter named Chloe and she was once two years old like the character in the book.

But then I realize that I'm wrong. I only ever had a brother I didn't know about and then another group of brothers I knew even less about.

Still, I know Chloe is different from Ursula because Chloe doesn't dress that way or talk that way or eat pie like that.

Even still I wish Ursula the best and I'm glad we don't know each other anymore and that she doesn't know my television doesn't work and neither does my telephone and I can't remember the last time I tasted pie or bourbon and that I'm freezing to death all alone in here.

What I'm saying is this is for Ursula and Chloe, my niece in the story and maybe in real life, too, if I ever had one, and by this I mean an imaginary bourbon because I have long since run out, which I raise in salute to both of them, alive or dead, working in a saloon or on a movie set or praying for anyone who might need it.

The Trouble with Paddling

The trouble with paddling is your arms get tired. I tell this to the girls sitting next to me but they don't listen. They say they don't have time and they're too busy but maybe make an appointment and we'll talk. They say we can get together for coffee sometime. I ask if they like pastries with their coffee but they tell me no, they say we don't like pastries. I tell them I don't like pastries either. I tell them I have a gluten sensitivity but they think I'm lying. You can tell they think I'm lying by the way they are standing and pointing at me and calling me a liar. This is why I don't like talking to girls on the subway. They don't know that eating a single pastry can land me back in the hospital and this time I might not get out. They don't know how much I love pastry and how I miss it. My mother would wake early in the morning to bake us pastries and that was breakfast for me growing up. There I'd be at the breakfast table and the sun was slowly waking up and the moon was fast asleep and I remember it was peaceful and I would eat my pastries in peace. These days there isn't a moment's peace, not in the morning or anytime. The problem is I think about the girls when I try to sleep at night and they keep me awake. Sometimes I say goodnight girls out loud even though they can't hear me and say goodnight back. These girls are exactly like the women who can't have children for the hateful look in their eyes. Last week when

I saw them on the subway it was horrible. All of them looking at a baby and wishing it dead. I couldn't see the baby from where I was sitting, but I understood. I was on my way home and hoping to make plans with Esperanza, who has been avoiding me of late. I don't know if Esperanza wants children of her own, as we aren't allowed to talk about anything that might upset her. This is a rule she made up and is adamant about. Once I asked about her job at the restaurant and she started crying. She said it was awful because of the pendejos in the back of the house, who never leave her alone, who were all of them swine. She said they make suggestive remarks and crude gestures and they fondle and grope her like they were politicians or movie producers. She said we are never to speak of it again. I can't remember the last time I saw Esperanza. In this respect she is like my mother, who I haven't seen in years. Some people ask if Esperanza reminds me of anyone and I answer no, but this isn't true. She could be a cousin or my Sofia or her beautiful yet elusive twin sister, Tanya. I think both are dead now and I want God to rest their ambushed souls. I want them to know peace, which is what I want for myself, too. I haven't been able to eat in peace since my mother, haven't been able to eat a pastry, either. The girls don't know about the peace at breakfast time. They don't know how many times I've been in the hospital and how the doctors tell me I should be careful or next time I might not make it out. They don't know about Esperanza or the women that can't have children. I don't tell them any of this because I'm trying to warn them about paddling, about how your arms get tired and if your arms get tired then it's goodnight maybe forever, but this is another thing they don't know anything about and what's worse is they don't even want to.

Even the Moonlight is Blinding

Manny said he didn't want anything he couldn't turn off and put in a closet. We were talking about if he wanted children, if he and his wife ever discussed such things. Manny said they didn't have anything in writing, but they'd taken measures. I didn't ask about the measures, but I know one or two things about his wife so I knew what he meant, what the measures entailed.

For my part, I've tried to stay away from anyone who might want to continue a conversation with me past its natural lifespan. Someone who could want something in writing.

Manny was over for the weekend. We hadn't seen each other in a few years, since the last time he was over for a weekend. We didn't keep up much during the intervals.

This morning Manny said he was hungry for breakfast. I'm almost never hungry for breakfast so I almost never eat it. I told him we could check out the farmer's market, that something like breakfast might turn up there. Django's been wanting to go to the farmer's market together, but that's something only real couples do.

At the market people were buying fish and vegetables and fruit and bread and everyone looked like they had purpose, like they knew what they wanted to eat for dinner that night, what they wanted to do with the rest of their lives. Otherwise, they looked like they were already dead and didn't have the sense to fall down yet.

I couldn't tell what Manny looked like, but he was one or the other.

Django and I have been at it for a few months now, mostly on the weekends. It's possible she wants to marry me and have children. It's also possible she'll want nothing to do with me come Christmas. I like that we never talk about it and it's all guesswork until we don't know each other anymore.

Until then and otherwise, it's mostly perfect.

At the market bona fide couples were pushing babies around in strollers and that's how the subject came up. Manny and I can get heavy after a few beers, but I don't remember ever talking about children before. I think I was the one who mentioned it first, because Manny was married now and I haven't seen him since it happened.

Manny said, I don't want anything I can't turn off and put in a closet.

I said, I don't even have a closet.

Then Manny said, I'll tell you what else I don't like. I don't like it when I recognize the old woman in a movie and I remember her as a young woman in another movie, one that doesn't seem old, one they made when I was a teenager.

I told him I knew what he meant. I said, it happens all the time now.

I asked him about music, if he missed it.

Why I asked is because people like Manny are meant to roam free and unencumbered, by wives and children and any kind of gainful employment. They're meant to write songs and sing them to people in dive bars and ride along on their genius until they destroy themselves.

Manny was the best guitar player I'd ever heard so what I'm talking about is a kind of American tragedy.

Manny said, I never think about it, don't have time.

I decided not to say anything, but liked to have beaten him with a stick.

Instead I asked him why he felt that way about children, if something happened.

Manny said, I don't like them, end of story.

I said, they lack perspective.

I said, people should stop having children now. Enough is enough.

Manny said, it has gone too far, both here in America and everywhere else.

I said, never to have been born is best.

There was a four-piece ensemble playing ragtime jazz for everyone at the market. Upright bass, a couple of horns, guitar. They sounded good, practiced. They had a guitar case out and open in front of them. Some compact discs and dollar bills littered it for decoration. Every so often one of the mothers or fathers would stop and listen, cajole the others in their party to do likewise.

Manny said to me, I don't know how you do it.

I said, I don't know how I do it, either.

Then time passed, enough for a slow mournful waltz to begin and end with a smattering of polite applause from mothers, fathers, children, zombies.

Then I said, what don't we know?

Manny said, living here, like this. Doing what you do with your life and women. Floating and buzzing. There has to be a better way.

I said, I'm sure you're right.

Manny said, what's this new one, Django?

I said, that's her, yes.

Manny said, is that her real name?

I said, I don't think so. I think she told me her real name the night we met, but I can't remember what it was.

Manny said, she's like the old woman in the movie.

What I love about Manny is we can have a full conversation and I'll walk away better and wiser for it, like I spent a long night in a nowhere town off Route 66, walked into a saloon and a fistfight with a stranger, fell in love with the bartender's woman, and ended up in the drunk tank. Come morning I'm turning new leafs over and changing my ways.

Manny has been alive for thousands of years and there's nothing he doesn't know, hasn't seen a hundred times before.

Manny said they have a farmer's market where he lives, but he never goes to it. He said he has his own garden and they grow more food than they know what to do with. He said he has to give away tomatoes and basil to the neighbors so it won't go to waste. He said there's something about this practice that bothers him. He said it's like communism.

This is when he said he was down ten grand on college football but he wasn't going to bet the games today. He said he was in a bad slump. I asked if he needed money, but then said I didn't have any to lend him.

Manny said, I borrowed some from a guy back home who's only juicing me two points a week. I should be square in a month or two.

I used to place bets through him years ago, but realized I didn't care enough about sports or money to keep at it.

I noticed some pretty mothers pushing ugly babies around. Everything about it seemed like a mistake to me. Like this isn't what the human race was meant to do, procreate indiscriminately and then behave like this in front of people that know better. That maybe it was our job to let everybody know this, to stand up and make a few things clear.

Manny and I were roommates once and this is how we've always talked to each other, but then he met his wife playing co-ed softball and they moved to one of those square states in the middle of the country no one cares about.

I didn't know he was still gambling. I think years ago he told me he was going to stop, but maybe he meant drinking. Back when we lived together he got himself into a number of holes, both with gambling and booze, but he'd always dig himself out. I only had to loan him money a few times and post bail once.

Manny said, we're speaking in hypotheticals now. We know this can't happen in real life.

I tracked a mother with curly hair from the fishmonger to the baker's table. I couldn't decide if she reminded me of anyone, perhaps a bad mistake or two.

Manny was talking about his marriage presently, the one he's been in for almost three years. I think the last thing he said was about his wife and how she folds everything. Towels and sheets and paper napkins, plastic bags, cardboard boxes, anything that can be folded.

I said, this is someone we arrange help for, we call in the Marines, the Red Cross.

Manny said, as a boy I dreamed of being a soldier and fighting overseas in a great world war. Didn't care who against, the commies in Russia, China, Cuba, any of those. I wanted one day to be a hero. I imagined myself in a trench, dug in, maintaining position until my relief came, which it never did.

He said, how come that never happened?

I said, because you married a folder.

We each took slugs of beer and watched the people collecting vegetables. There was a long line for summer squash and radicchio. I buy my vegetables at the supermarket, but only if they're on sale and there's no line.

I said, this sounds like the movie the old lady was in when she was younger. I asked him why he never joined the Army.

He said he couldn't remember the details. He remembers trying to enlist, filling out the paperwork, taking a physical. But they failed him, said there was something wrong with his heart, it skipped beats or murmured or something.

Manny had a straight job when we lived together so we were rarely around at the same time. I had come into family money and lived off of it until I couldn't anymore. Then I had to work in a restaurant two or three nights a week.

I don't know what his business is exactly, but I'm sure he's explained it to me more than once. He tells people what to do and they do it, something about books and schools, educational materials. Sometimes he flies to other cities and tells people what to do there. That's what he was doing here this weekend. He had a meeting on Friday and made the weekend of it. I remembered he still owed me five hundred dollars for an amplifier.

Our plan was for us to go to a party later that night, after the farmer's market and dinner, if we were to have dinner. Manny didn't like parties, but I told him no one does.

He asked me how I knew the host, what kind of party it was.

I told him it was the friend of a friend and something to do, that we can kill time and save lives. I told him the house is always darker than it should be, that it seems like they forgot to pay the electric bill, but you can see everything you need to.

Manny said, even the moonlight is blinding out here.

I said, the key is not looking up.

There was an old woman next to us who was telling everyone what they were doing wrong. She told a young mother to fold up a blanket and stick it inside the stroller. She told a second mother that her daughter was unhappy and wanted to walk around on her own. Finally, she admonished one redheaded child for stealing the hobbyhorse of another. I was waiting for her to get around to the two of us, drinking beer in the middle of the day and talking about what's best left unsaid.

Manny said, this is what's left of America, right here.

I said, they should give it back to the Indians.

Manny said, it's an asylum.

I said, and it's done for like the rest of us.

Manny said, I worry about you sometimes.

I don't like summer because the mothers of America are everywhere with bare legs and shoulders and toes all out in the open. I don't like it because this is what it does to people like Manny, people like me. We're made to sit and watch the calamity instead of doing what we're supposed to do out on the road, making music and memories we'll struggle to recall for years to come.

It's probably a good idea I'd never been to a farmer's market before and the almost naked women make it all worse. Django always catches me looking whenever we're out together. I feel bad sometimes, but I think she knows I can't help it.

I think Manny is the same way. I see him inspecting each one as she walks by—a parade of nobody's business, is what he calls it.

I'm not sure I believe that Manny worries about me. Maybe because I don't worry about him even though he's always on the brink of ruin.

It was after we polished off the six-pack that Manny said he'd catch up with me later. This is something that Manny does whenever he is in town. He likes to go off and do his own thing and then I usually don't hear from him until he's at the airport.

I always figure he's at a track or casino, but that's his own business.

I reminded him about the party. I told him that we should get there around nine if we get there at all.

I took the opportunity to go home and nap, but that didn't work because the electric company has been tearing up the street for three weekends in a row. Every time that jackhammer sounds off I consider committing violent crimes, but instead I shove earplugs into myself and try to find something to do. I'd been putting together some songs but they weren't going anywhere. Some had good melodies but no lyrics, others had good chord progressions but nothing else.

I decided to shower and shave and go see Django but then I cut my head shaving. I did what I could to staunch the bleeding but nothing worked and then I lost motivation.

I didn't tell Django about the party because that would defeat the purpose. And I'm sure she had her own party to go to with the same idea in mind, to find someone better, someone else, someone to go to the market with, listen to jazz and buy fish.

I told her I'd like to see her tomorrow, but mentioned that Manny was in town and having a hard time and I should be there for him. I told her he was having marital problems and there was something wrong with his garden. She said it was fine, said another time then. I told her I cut my head and couldn't get it to stop bleeding.

At the party I met someone who reminded me of Manny, then I met someone that reminded me of Django. I don't know where the real Manny was but I'm sure he was fine and Django was probably fine, too. I talked to both stand-ins for an hour each, learned about who they were and what they did and where they'd been and how it was all going. One said we should meet for coffee sometime and I said why not because I knew it would never happen. They seemed like good people, but maybe they weren't. Maybe one was a horse thief and the other a loan shark. You can never tell from one conversation.

The Dahlberg Repercussions

The woman on the subway looked like my mother so I sat down next to her and said you look like my mother. I said does it seem like that to you, that you are someone who looks like my mother and that I look like someone who could be your son, if circumstances were different, that is, if you were old enough to be my mother or I were young enough to be your son. I said don't misunderstand me. I said you look like how my mother used to look, not how she looks now, although my mother still looks good and I didn't mean to imply otherwise. I said my mother is a good-looking woman and that bodes well for all of us. I'm talking about genes now more than anything else. The truth is I haven't seen my mother in twenty years because she won't have anything more to do with me. So when I said my mother looks good now it's only speculation. I remember her own mother, my grandmother that is, and she kept her looks well into her seventies. This is when the woman who looked like my mother said, excuse me, sir, and I admonished her for being so formal. I said how dare you with someone that could be your son if circumstances were different. I could tell she was from a better class of people by the way she spoke and what she wore and thus could never be my mother, but I kept on anyway. This is when the woman who looked like my mother got up from the bench and walked over to the doors.

She stood there staring straight into her own reflection and waiting for the next stop. She looked like a flagpole in an open field to me. It looked like she couldn't be toppled, like she was entirely unmovable, and that she would never acknowledge that she was someone who looked like my mother or that I was someone who could be her son.

Roy-Boy

I used to call him Roy-boy, not for any other reason than I liked the sound of it, those two monosyllabic words up against each other and rhyming like a boxer's one-two punch, a jab and a cross, coming down square on the chin, and there were rumors he liked men and I never wanted to confuse him because I didn't like men or at least I didn't like them the way Roy-boy was rumored to like them, but I also wanted him in my corner because he worked the back of the house and I needed him to do things for me, get things, fix things, assemble things, so I never minded if Roy-boy thought I liked him and he seemed like a good guy and I didn't care about the rumors, and even when people asked what I thought about Roy-boy I'd say I don't think anything, and they'd ask why I called him Roy-boy because everyone called him either Roy or Chico, even his older brother Jorge, who got him the job and was in charge of the back of the house, and I'd tell them how I liked the sound of it, the one-two punch, and I don't think they ever believed me, I think they thought there was more to it but I didn't care because I liked Esperanza who worked in the front of the house with me, and she knew the truth or she would know it if I ever got her alone, which never happened and I still don't know why because it was clear she liked me too but then something spooked her and you can never tell with women, which is something you'd hear from the back of the house all the time, even Roy-boy, who I liked best out of all of them because he'd always have a smile on his face whenever you went back there to ask him to fix or assemble something, not like the rest of them, Jorge and the others, who would curse you in Spanish and call you maricon if you asked them to do anything and this was especially true when they found out I was half Rican and couldn't speak the language, they would ask me a question in mile-a-minute Spanish and I'd sing the lyrics to Oye Como Va in response, which was the only Spanish I knew, so you know they hated my guts but they hated everyone in the front of the house, they'd throw tortillas and ladles at you when you crossed through the kitchen but you couldn't blame them because it was awful working back there, that rotten stale stench getting into your body and coming out of your pores, the heat bouncing off the walls and there was nowhere to hide except maybe the walk-in and you couldn't last long in there no matter how hot it was, and every time you went back there you had to hold your breath and try not to let those bastards get to you, like how they'd harass all the women, including Esperanza, who was their favorite because of the tight skirts and sweaters, and they'd drop utensils on the floor so she'd have to bend over to pick them up and they'd all hoot and holler and then everyone would laugh and laugh, including Esperanza, who was a good sport even with those pendejos which was one of the reasons I always liked her, until everyone went too far and got carried away but we aren't permitted to talk about that so let's say she was always classy, never went along when I told Jorge and the rest of them that two ICE agents were in the house asking questions, he even mentioned you by name, Jorge, how do you like that, bueno pa' gozar mi amigo, and to this day I don't know what might've spooked her, except to say that one night when we closed together and had a couple of drinks in the bar after work I asked her a question and she answered by saying oh, my goodness, and we don't know each other well enough, and then I may've made a suggestion or two of how we could get to know each other better and I think I remember her asking if it was true what they said about Chico and I said I didn't know and more than that I didn't care and what you have to remember is this was a long time ago and for someone not to care about that sort of thing was considered suspicious back then, even with Esperanza, who despite being a good sport was just like the rest of them in most respects, even though she would smile at me and bat her eyes and feel my muscles and ask how I kept in such good shape so I'd tell her that I'd turned my mother's basement into a gym and I'd work out every night for at least two hours and I used to play tennis professionally and she'd smile again and bat again and so I thought maybe it could happen with Esperanza but the upshot was nothing ever happened, nothing at all, not with Esperanza in the front of the house nor with Roy-boy in the back of it and I can't remember who stopped working there first, if it was Esperanza who went on to marry one of the regulars, some retired detective who'd come in to bother her every night around closing and everyone liked him or at least tolerated him, but I could tell he thought he was better than all of us by the way he called people kid or sweetheart, and so I called him out on it once and there was something of a dustup, we had to take it outside, and I was ready to drop that motherfucker with the lightning-quick one-two combination I'd been practicing on the heavy bag in my mother's basement, before Roy-boy and the others broke it up, everyone saying it wasn't worth it and I was nothing if not cool back then so everyone walked away, which was a shame because I would've loved dropping that motherfucker but by then I decided this was Esperanza's problem and if this is what she wanted it was vaya con huevos for her, they deserve each other, and Esperanza wound up quitting two weeks later and then Roy-boy flat out disappeared, he stopped showing up for work one day and Jorge, his brother, would never say whatever happened to him or where he went or even if he was dead or alive and I tried asking a couple of times but I didn't want it to seem like I cared that much because I didn't really, I just liked saying his name out loud and he's the only Roy I've ever known and I'm not sure if I were to meet another Roy if I'd call that one Roy-boy, too, I guess it would depend if that guy seemed like a Roy-boy, which Roy-boy always did, if that makes sense, and I like to think that Roy-boy is still around somewhere, that he's working in the back of a better house and the people there haven't heard the rumors about him, whether they're true or not.

Two Syndromes at Once

A Mongoloid baby is crying on the subway and so now everyone is a hostage. Everyone is sitting next to or across from the baby or standing up and away from it but we might as well be bound and gagged in the back of a gas station. We look at each other like we don't know what is happening but it's undeniable that we want this baby dead or to stop crying so we can go back to the magazine we are reading or the music we are listening to or the frayed hem of the skirt we're eviscerating. Everyone feels badly about this, about wanting this baby dead or to stop crying because it is a Mongoloid baby and it is the middle of the day. Perhaps if it were early morning or late at night people would feel differently and yes, it's true, everyone knows you're not supposed to call this kind of baby a Mongoloid anymore, but this is what we call him. When I say this is what we call him I mean this is what I call him. Sometimes I assume what happens to me happens to everyone or what I think occurs to everyone. Sometimes I make that mistake. The world goes away whenever I sleep or turn my back, which is why I make that mistake, I think. It's the same mistake God makes. God always thinks he's God, that's his problem. I can tell everyone agrees with me both about God and this baby and that maybe if this baby weren't a Mongoloid everyone would feel differently, but there's no way of knowing. We believe most people don't want to be around a crying baby regardless if it's a Mongoloid or not and no matter what time of day it is either. What some people don't know is the doctor who they named this syndrome after was an awful human being and his thoughts on the whys and wherefores of this condition are just as offensive as calling the baby a Mongoloid in the first place. We tell this to the mother and then we tell her we have nothing against the Mongolians as a people and that we respect Genghis Khan as much as anyone. We might even mention that millions of people are related to both Genghis Khan and his brother, Don, and that is impressive no matter how you look at it. We tell her we are not here to judge anyone and then we ask what is the baby's name and does he always cry like this in public. The woman looks at us and says, how dare you. We don't know how to respond so we apologize. We say that we don't mean to upset her. We feel sorry for this woman and it's possible we are already in love with her. It's possible we have profound feelings for this woman because of what she has to go through every day and also she is pretty and has nice hair and toes. This makes us wonder about the father and what his problem is and if he is in the picture. We'd bet his name is Don and we'd bet this woman has been looking for a way out since she met him. She feels trapped and who could blame her. This is when we realize we might be suffering from Stockholm syndrome and we ask each other if this is what is happening. One of us says we have two syndromes going on at once if such is the case. Meanwhile the baby keeps crying and when we say crying we mean screaming more than anything else. It's as if the baby is on the rack or is being disemboweled or something likewise unimaginable. We want to ask if the mother is taking the baby to the hospital, but we don't because the mother would take this the wrong way. We wonder if the father is out now with another woman, one who doesn't have a baby and might, in fact, be barren so this kind of travesty could never happen again. This is another thing

we don't tell to the mother, who by now is cursing at us while covering the baby's ears and rocking it back and forth. By now we know
this woman is past saving and there's nothing we can do, so this is
when we get off at the next stop even though we are supposed to take
this train to the end of the line. I'm still not sure why I say we when
I'm the only one who thinks this way or says anything about it out
loud. I probably shouldn't do that. I probably should stay quiet about
what I think and assume and the mistakes both God and I make.

Three Kinds of People on the Crosstown Bus

Sometimes I don't make it out of the house. When I tell people this in the way of conversation, in the way human people can sometimes spill onto each other in broad daylight, they try hard to change the subject.

When I am in the house I watch television. I almost never do anything but watch television in the house. I do sleep and shower. I have a great shower in my house and if I'm not watching the television then that's where you'll find me. Sometimes I eat, yes, usually twice a day, something that stands in for breakfast around noontime, perhaps boiled eggs and toast, and then again in the evening, which is usually catch as catch can. Maybe I open some soup or I order takeout and have it delivered. It never gets in the way of the television, though. I scan the channels from 2 to 80 and back again, whether I'm eating or not. I spend five or so seconds on each station. What's on television isn't important to me. That I am looking for something else is what matters. I am a seeker.

I seek.

What I have never sought is a job watching television. I've also never sought fame or fortune, acceptable living conditions, or Trina, but I'm not ready to think about Trina right now. Trina has her place and it isn't here and now.

Trina says she only recently got a television herself, that for years she went without one. I have no idea how she spent time or what her life was like.

This is one reason I'm not ready to think about her.

Sometimes I am forced to leave the house and it's always a tragedy when this happens. Sometimes I am compelled to show up at a certain place at a certain time and perform certain tasks for several hours at a time and after that I take the most direct route back to the house and television.

I have to take a bus to get to the certain place at the certain time. What happens is I rouse myself with great difficulty, shower, shave, eat something regrettable, dress, and vacate the house. I do all of this in fifteen minutes. I understand other people need an hour or so to do this, which is something I've never understood.

The buses in this city make a horrible noise when they stop. Sometimes my head comes off my shoulders when I hear it. I have to cover my ears with both hands to keep this from happening. People look at me when I do this. I can't tell what they might think.

The people at the bus stop are a troubled class of people. They have troubles at home and troubles at work. Except not all of them have homes or jobs and these people are even more troubled. You never see these kinds of people on television, though as I think this I realize it's wrong. You do see these kinds of people on television these days, but I always choose not to watch them.

Mostly it's the troubled people and old ladies that ride the bus in this city. Most are fat and they are usually nice people, these fat ones, though that is not always the case, either. Sometimes when I start a thought I'll think it correct only to realize halfway through that it isn't. The trouble is one doesn't always have the time to think things through. This is what happened with Trina, as a case in point.

Some of them, yes, the fat ones, they are nice people, except for the ones who aren't, but who cares in the end. Some of them are colleagues, I think. I can't say for sure as I don't ever speak to my colleagues, except for Trina, starting with the time I said after you at the coffee pot.

Trina is likewise fat and I suppose now is the time to mention her.

Trina is my immediate supervisor at work and the one who hired me. At the coffee pot she uses a lot of cream and almost always takes two doughnuts back to her office. I never see her eating the doughnuts, though one assumes that's what she does.

Trina doesn't mind being fat, I don't think. Sometimes you can tell that sort of thing about certain people by the way they walk around the world, how they carry themselves, what they wear, how they feed, covering their mouths as they chew, as if saying I don't normally do this, but I can't help it, I'm sorry.

I never eat this way even though I'm fat as well. But my weight bounces up and down and so sometimes I'm not as fat as I am now.

Also, I'm a man and no one cares that I'm fat and neither do I.

Trina walks around like everyone else, carries herself erect and properly, with a certain elegance, wears clothes that befit her architecture, and all the rest.

I would even call her beautiful because pretty works no matter what. She said once that she's a proud big, beautiful woman and I agreed with her by looking at the floor and keeping quiet.

What happened was she came up to my cubicle and asked me what I was doing after work. I'd been working for this same firm for six months and no one had asked me what I was doing afterwards. It felt like I was being interrogated, that I was suspected of some criminal misdoing. I asked her what she meant and she said follow me.

We wound up in her office and she closed the door. I sat down in the chair in front of her desk. At this point I was hoping the fire alarm would ring. Sometimes the fire alarm rings and everyone has to evacuate the building.

This is when she said where are you from. I told her I was born and raised in the city and then she asked about my heritage. I told her I was half Rican and half something else and she said I like Latin men best. She said that she was part Dominican but I'm not sure I believed her. She is fair-skinned and doesn't speak with an accent and I never heard her speak any Spanish, which is the exact opposite of every Dominican I've seen on television.

Then she said I am taking you to dinner. I said, are you sure? Then she didn't say anything after that. She had a strange look on her face and her right arm had disappeared between her legs, but I couldn't tell what she might be doing as the desk obstructed my view. For this I was grateful. A minute or two later she said I had great shoulders and it looked like I lifted weights, which isn't true.

Years ago I would work out in my mother's basement, but I haven't seen her or her basement in ages.

I've forgotten what was for dinner or if it was enjoyable. I rarely enjoy eating at a restaurant. There are always too many people and something always goes wrong and then you are left to pay for others' mistakes. Also, I was too busy trying to think of things to say, questions I should ask. I thought I had to act a certain way, otherwise she would fire me. I didn't actually care about being fired, but then I'd have to find another job and there's almost nothing worse than looking for a job.

Trina seemed functional, she laughed some, smiled some, asked me questions about work, about home, about what I like to do, about how I grew up. I think I answered most of the questions honestly. She didn't need to know about my mother and father, how they took turns leaving and raising me, what they did for a living. I don't think I've told anyone about growing up because it wasn't as bad as it sounds.

I told her I like to watch television and take showers. She said she preferred baths, but it was more fun bathing with someone else. I told her I only had a stall in my house, but it was a good one. I told her about the water pressure and the tile and this is when she beckoned the waiter for more wine and said no one cares about water pressure.

We didn't have dessert because sometimes fat people don't like to have dessert in front of each other.

I didn't tell her that I eat pie almost every day.

I didn't tell her that I diet sometimes but always stop because what's the difference.

After dinner she took me home. I settled into the left corner of the sofa as she moved about the ground floor. I didn't know what she was doing but I was happy to be left alone. I was hoping to collect my thoughts, consider what had taken place and what was likely to happen next. I was hoping to find a way out and back home to the television. I could still watch for an hour or two before bed. I can't fall asleep unless I watch an hour or two of television and I need to sleep every night for at least ten hours.

The truth is I had no idea what Trina wanted with me, if anything. I hadn't been in a house other than my own in a long time and wasn't sure of the protocol. She'd said I should make myself comfortable before she disappeared into the kitchen. I didn't know what this should entail, if this meant I should remove my jacket or the rest of my clothing. So I loosened my tie, and if pressed about it I would've said this is how I get comfortable. I would've told her that I am so rarely comfortable that it isn't usually worth the bother.

What happened next was I think we had sexual intercourse. There was a time there, while watching a horror movie and without warning, that she climbed atop me and removed her undergarments. Before that we were side by side on the sofa. There was no contact while we were side by side, though she did remove the throw pillow barrier I'd constructed. I think she said something like we won't need this. I think I said something like whatever you say. She'd brought two glasses of wine in from the kitchen earlier and set them down on the coffee table in front of the sofa. This is where she placed the pillow, next to the wine on the coffee table. On the screen there was all kinds of carnage, a lunatic mutilating young women indiscriminately, I think. I couldn't tell exactly what was happening because the volume was low and I couldn't hear the dialogue.

After she'd made herself comfortable on my lap, she reached for my belt buckle and unbuckled it. Then she fished me out of my shorts and began manipulating. I tried looking around her to the screen, but it was difficult. She was especially wide on my lap like this. I think the lunatic was hiding in a basement at this point, unbeknownst to the homeowners. I think he was about to lay waste to an entire family.

I didn't want to look down. I could feel what she was doing, but I didn't want to see it. I think she said very nice while she was handling me and I said thank you.

This is when she took a breath. I didn't know what was expected, if I should say something. I had my hands flat against the sofa and my feet firm against the floor. I waited for something to happen, for the fire alarm to go off, for one of us to die of a heart attack. I'd seen it on television, people dying of heart attacks in the middle like this. I figured if it was me Trina could be charged with the crime, but they couldn't hold me responsible for Trina, given my position relative to hers.

Trina's eyes were closed and it seemed like she was about to pass out.

I said to her, are you okay?

She said, don't talk.

I sat still.

She began to move, rocking back and forth, as if I were a hobbyhorse. The sensation was not unpleasant, though at one point my thighs began to burn. I had my hands around her waist or what I thought was her waist. I figured she needed support and I didn't want her to fall off. She kept her head down the whole time, like she was trying to keep track of something. The rocking went on for quite some time. I wanted to look at my watch but I didn't want to take my hands off her sides. The movie was over and another had started on the screen I could barely see. I don't know what happened to the lunatic or the family he was about to slaughter.

I knew we were finished when she stopped the rocking, slapped me across the face, and started convulsing. The convulsions went on for about a minute and then she calmed herself and her breathing became regular. She hung her head, and for a second or two I thought she had died, that I was going to have to explain myself to the authorities after all, tell them that we were coworkers, tell them about the coffee pot, the dinner, the pillow barrier I'd constructed. This is when she looked up at me and made eye contact. She looked broken, done in.

I said, are you okay?

She said, we're going to have to do that again.

I said, are you sure?

She said, I am.

There is a neighbor that is always outside the building and always unavoidable when I am on my way to the certain place in the godless morning.

I don't know what he does or how he lives. He wears the appropriate clothes for the weather, but there is something wrong with him. He calls me Boss.

I never introduced myself as Boss and he has never expressed a desire to be my subordinate. What I call him is Hey There. Hey There doesn't resemble anyone at the certain place so he's probably not confusing me with a superior. I am no one's superior, not at work, not anywhere in the world. At the certain place my responsibilities are menial. I do what I do and every so often Trina comes by and fondles me or makes a suggestive comment. There is no one beneath me there and I am never up for a promotion or due for a raise.

I am always beneath Trina because this is how she likes it, both in and out of the office.

Trina has never met Hey There and when I referenced him once in conversation she had no idea who I was talking about.

This morning Hey There was outside the building and said something like some weather we're having and I said something like tell me about it.

Trina is the same way. The first thing she'll say in the morning concerns the weather and it's my job to agree with her. People always need confirmation, assurance. They need to know that they're not completely insane, that someone sees the world the same as them. In truth, I don't know what people take or what they need, but this is what I have figured out so far from watching television.

Trina takes me out of my pants whenever she pleases but I doubt she actually needs to do so. I don't think anyone's life depends on it.

The weather here is always like the weather here and everyone knows it.

Sometimes, when I remain in the house for a few days, Trina will call on the phone to check on me. She wants to know if I am still alive, if I'm sick, what's wrong. I made the mistake of answering once. I told her, yes, I was still alive and that I was indeed sick. I told her I had bronchitis and that it was contagious. I told her it felt like I was choking to death and that my chest hurt. She told me she missed my face. I'd never heard this expression before, missing someone's face, either in real life or on television. Regardless, I didn't believe her as there's nothing about my face anyone can miss. I have the same parts as most people, two eyes on either side of a nondescript nose, lips, teeth. My face is like a sheet of paper. I coughed into the phone and then apologized for doing so and then said I had to go lie down. Now I let the phone ring when I know it's going to be her.

On the bus I try to find a seat against a window, preferably a single, but it's almost always hopeless. The troubled ones always take up the best seats. I listen to them talk to each other. I spend about five seconds on each before I start listening to the next person.

When I arrive at work, I go straight to my cubicle. They have a cubicle for me here and I sit inside of it. There is a desk and on top of the desk is a computer. My task is to read things on the computer and make sense of it. I type up reports and send them to certain people. These are the superiors. Once in a while one of them comes by to ask a question. Sometimes I have the answer. When I don't have the answer I say I'll have to get back to them.

I almost had to get back to them about what happened on the bus once. A troubled no-account slid in next to me and started right away with what he's afraid of. He didn't say hello, didn't introduce himself. He started listing his fears, one after another. He mentioned how he's afraid of pigeons, afraid of waking up too late, afraid of alarm clocks, spaghetti, and so forth. He talked about his mother, how she was the one who taught him to be afraid like this. Said she was afraid of sour milk, dried leaves, houseplants, pancake batter, postcards, nail clippers, file cabinets. His mother was dead now, said she died five years ago and now it's her ghost he's afraid of.

I didn't recognize this man, but he was one of them, one who rides the bus back and forth all the time. Every time we approached a stop I was hoping he'd get off but he didn't. He kept going on and on about what scared him, about toy poodles and wilted spinach. It was after he mentioned helicopters that he looked over at me and squinted. I told him that my superior was sexually harassing me at work. I figured he needed to hear something like that, something that might make him feel better, make him count blessings and go away.

He didn't care about my superior or the harassment. Instead he talked about the weather, how he was afraid of the bitter cold and sunstroke and tornadoes. I told him he was right, that I was afraid of these things too. I told him sometimes I don't make it out of the house. I told him I don't know how to act around other people and this is why I prefer the television. This is when I got off the bus. I was already one stop past where I normally get off and would have to walk all the way back.

That was the only conversation I've had with someone on the bus. I started to tell Trina about it once, but she was about to change the rhythm of her motion so I decided not to.

I don't know how much longer this business will go on with Trina, but I think it's out of my hands, unless I stay home for the rest of my life.

So this is what I'm going to do.

I haven't been out of the house in two weeks and it's only the beginning. I don't think anything will get me to leave again, not a fire, not a hurricane or tornado, not eviction.

I have everything I need and by this I mean the television and shower.

I have cans of soup and there's takeout and delivery.

Should the phone ring I'll let it keep ringing until it stops or I have to unplug it from the wall.

Should Trina knock on my door I'll pretend that I'm dead or don't live here anymore.

Should anyone ask I'll say what's the difference.

To Grow Old in America

On the subway an old man is looking at a young woman and it's clear he wants to fuck or kill her or fuck her and then kill her or kill her and then fuck her. I am here to tell you I think this is awful. This old man is quite old and I should think he wouldn't want to fuck or kill anyone anymore. I should think that at his age he has killed and fucked enough to satisfy himself or anyone else. I want to tell this to the person next to me but the person next to me is almost as old as the old man so I decide against it. But this particular old person is a woman and she is not looking at anything. She has her eyes closed and is thinking about God knows what. I don't want to speculate as to what this woman is thinking about because I'm sure it will drag us further down. I want to ask her if this is what I have to look forward to. I want to say that if this is what it means to grow old in America I want no part of it. I don't want to look at young women with murderous and lustful intent or sit quietly with my eyes closed thinking about God knows what when this is going on all around me. By the time I'm old the weather will be unbearably hot or cold because it's an ice age and the fascists will regain power and there'll be no more social security and everyone will have to work until they drop dead at their desks. God knows what will happen to what's left of America but he probably won't have to spend time blessing it anymore. People might realize by then that God never did bless America in the first place, that they've been singing the wrong song for years. This is probably why the old man wants to fuck and kill people all the time. He knows what's coming and is lucky he won't live to see it. The truth is I was on my way to see a friend and I was trying to remember what I should say to him. He called me yesterday to say he might check himself into a rehabilitation center. He said I should visit him during visiting hours. He's been having a tough time of it lately, lost his job and his pet dog and his grasp on what they call reality. The old woman doesn't know this about me or my friend and she probably wouldn't care if I told her. The same goes for the old man, unless I were someone he'd want to fuck or kill, which I'm sure I'm not. No one wants to fuck or kill me, which is one of my biggest problems. This is the whole subway ride until the young woman gets off at Fourteenth Street and the old man tries to find someone else to look at like this. I'm not sure if I'd be permitted to shoot him in the face because no one wants an old man behaving this way on the train. Meanwhile the old woman next to me still has her eyes closed so I'll never have any idea who she wants to fuck or kill or what she might be thinking or if she is as outraged as I am by all of it.

The Sexual Ramifications of Coffee

The thinking is maybe Betty has a single friend who wants sexual intercourse. This is why I'm meeting her for coffee. I myself don't drink coffee. I don't think Betty knows that I don't drink coffee, that I'm meeting her for another reason. I don't think Betty herself wants sexual intercourse because Betty is married. I've never met her husband so I can't say for sure that she is married. Sometimes people say they are married without actually being married. This is how it worked with my parents. My father was the one who said something about the institution, said it was passé, but this was before God found him. That's how he put it, that God found him, not the other way around like everybody else.

Once God found him, though, he got himself lost and we didn't see him again for a long time.

My mother would never use a word like passé, as it was beneath her. I can't remember her saying much except that there was a time for talking and a time for eating but never both at the same time. She said it wasn't American, said if I wanted to do both I should move to Europe or Mexico or someplace like that.

I'm not sure how I'll ask Betty if she has a single woman friend that might want sexual intercourse. It might take either audacity or finesse.

I'm not sure how or when I met Betty. I think it involved a social function and we have run into each other at other functions since that first one. It may've been a rally or a fundraiser. I think she is the director of an organization that helps women, keeps them from being exploited or harassed or helps them get elected to public office. It was at one of these that she suggested we meet for coffee sometime. It's possible she thought of me as a potential ally because she thinks I work for a senator, which I don't think was ever true.

She didn't say when she would like to meet so I assumed it would never happen. This is the kind of thing people say at social functions. No one means it when they say we should meet for coffee. People say we should meet for coffee when they are done talking with you and wish to talk with someone else. There's nothing immoral or unethical about this sort of lie. It's not like in Europe or Mexico, where people have no sense of decorum. This is what my mother told me. I think it was because her family was European or Mexican and she wished all of them dead.

My mother secretly hates that I'm half Puerto Rican, but it's her own fault for procreating with my father.

I'm not sure if Betty knows I'm half Rican. Sometimes women like this about me. They make certain assumptions about passion and other stereotypes.

When they find out I don't speak Spanish they are inconsolable.

I don't like how coffee tastes, bitter and sharp, but people don't know this, particularly the ones who invite me out to coffee at social functions.

Betty said we should meet for coffee three or four times before she meant it, which proves my point.

My mother was the opposite. She'd never repeat herself, never said something she didn't mean. Growing up I wasn't allowed to ask questions. All the time she would say, I'm not to be questioned. She'd even say this when I asked for help with my homework.

Instead she would dress me up and take my picture. She would have me assume different poses and tell me I should look scared, consumptive, hungry, surprised, seductive. She even put makeup on me, which I never cared for, but never said so out loud.

She never let me look at the photographs or the ones she took of my friends and neighbors. More than a few looked like me and I always wondered if we were related.

I don't know if Betty has children or how she dresses them up for photographs.

I am looking for sex for two reasons but only one is obvious. The other is Esperanza. I'm not sure I'd want her to know that I'm having sexual intercourse with someone else or if she'd even care.

I don't know why Betty wants to meet for coffee.

Betty's never indicated that she might want sexual intercourse but you can't always tell a thing like that. Sometimes you think a woman wants sex and it turns out she doesn't and other times you think a woman doesn't want sex and it turns out she does. This is one of the reasons people say what they say about women, both in story and song and polite conversation.

This is what happened with Esperanza. Sometimes it was yes and other times no and I could never tell which was which until she got married to the guy from the restaurant. And even then I couldn't tell on account of what she wore and how she walked and what she said both to me and other people.

I tried hard to keep my hands to myself but it was never easy.

If Betty does indeed want sex I will have to make a decision. I don't like disappointing people and I don't like making decisions. This is why I always modeled for my mother whenever she wanted to take my picture. Also, she'd threaten me, so I never had much choice.

I don't want to compromise Betty's marriage, though who knows if having intercourse with her would compromise her marriage. Perhaps both she and her husband are free to have coffee and sex with whomever they like.

Although my parents never said so out loud, this was the arrangement they had, I'm almost certain. I never saw one or the other with another man or woman, but I never saw much of either anyway.

I don't like to meet people's husbands as a rule. This way options are kept open. If I had to guess, though, I would say that Betty doesn't have this kind of marriage if she is married at all. Regardless, I suppose I will have sex with her if this is what she wants because I am a man and it's hard to say no to sex with someone who looks like Betty. People who look like Betty are exactly the ones you want to have sexual intercourse with. They have the hair and skin and everything is in proportion with everything else. They walk around like they own the world because they do.

These people don't care about you because everyone knows you're replaceable.

But this is not the reason I am meeting her for coffee. If nothing else, I want to make that much clear. I don't know anything about Betty and would never presume anything, either. And I'm not the sort of person who meets married women for coffee with this in mind.

This Is Me After Dance Class

It had been one month since we'd met, so it was okay for her to clean and redecorate my apartment is what I hear one snowdrop tell another on the subway. How you can tell they are snowdrops is the way they talk and dress and that the city is full of snowdrops now. I am on my way to the restaurant where Esperanza works but I'm not sure why. Maybe I want to see her through the glass, hustling drinks and appetizers. Maybe I want to see her fending off Jorge and the rest of the pendejos. I have my gun with me but I don't think I'll shoot her in the face. I can't say the same about her new husband if he is there. One snowdrop says, she said she'd wanted to do this since the first time she came over, the night we met at someone's going-away party. I've forgotten who was going away or where it was they were going. A mutual friend asked me to a party and I said yes, and so this is how we met and why it was okay for her to clean and redecorate my apartment. She said there's something wrong with me. She said she could see spending the rest of her life with me, but that doesn't mean something isn't wrong. This is when I want to tell the snowdrops about Esperanza, that she used to tell me that there was something wrong with me, but never said she could spend the rest of her life with me. I decide not to because snowdrops don't like it when you interrupt them. So the snowdrop continues and says, I told her it was true. I told her that I'm allergic to dust, that if I tried dusting I could have an anaphylactic reaction. She said that doesn't sound right to me. I want to say that it doesn't sound right to me, either, that I have allergies, too, but not like this. But we're talking about a snowdrop here. They are a gluten free range, artisanal, grass-fed organic people, so I don't say anything. I look out the window and track an old man walking an old dog on the platform. I don't recognize the man or the dog, can't tell who might be allergic to what. I also can't tell if I'm going to make it to the restaurant later. I might decide to get off at a different stop and do something else. I don't think I need to see Esperanza through the glass, see Jorge acting the fool and the rest of them, too. This way I won't have to shoot anyone in the face and won't have to explain it to the police afterwards. This is when I hear the snowdrop again. He says, she told me I shouldn't be alarmed. She said, this is me after dance class. I always have an abundance of energy. Can you believe it, an abundance of energy. I told her I wasn't kidding. I said, my throat could close and I could suffocate and die. She looked at me straight in the eye, did a pirouette. She said, that isn't the half of it. I considered what that could mean, the implications. This is when I decide I've had enough. I get up and stand directly over the two snowdrops sitting down. I stare right down at them until one of them is about to cry or say something slanderous. Then I tell them I don't know fractions, either, and I get off the train.

Woodpecker Pie for Christmas

They opened the store with a going-out-of-business sale. They were them, a man and woman, whatever. Maybe they were married, maybe divorced, maybe it doesn't make a difference. We can assign them names, Bill and Sharon, but it wouldn't matter. It wouldn't matter to them, the man and woman, and it wouldn't matter to Bill and Sharon, whoever they are.

This is the story my mother told me whenever she dressed me up to take my picture. I think she meant it as a distraction because she knew I didn't like it when she dressed me up, especially when she put the makeup on.

The man and woman had overheard someone talking at a bad luck bar that a Christmas store, selling ornaments and trees and lights, was a can't miss. Said you only had to work one month out of the year.

The man and woman had opened other stores and watched them go out of business before, a laundromat, a delicatessen, a haberdashery.

My mother said once it was a puppy mill. But then sometime around the holidays the puppies all died, probably of distemper. That sort of thing changes most people, and Bill and Sharon, if those are their names, were no exception.

For a long while I wondered if Bill and Sharon were my mother and father. I think I remember that my father did something with animals before God found him and he left us. But the Sharon character never seemed like my mother, for a lot of reasons I don't have the stomach to go into. But that doesn't mean it wasn't her in disguise.

On the other side of town from the store, in a modest house, Sharon sits on a loveseat. There is no one sitting next to her. There is no room for anyone to sit next to her as the loveseat can only accommodate one at a time. In fact, it is not a loveseat at all, but this is what she calls it. She has her legs folded beneath her. She is comfortable. She is not reading or watching television. She is not knitting or listening to music. Perhaps later she will go for a walk around the block.

She should be at the store right now, taking care of the register or helping customers, but she isn't. She's in the loveseat.

Her husband is down on Division hawking trees and tinsel. His name might be Bill and he might be her ex-husband by now. They have been married and divorced to each other several times over.

This is one of those details that reminded me of my mother and father. Even if they weren't officially married and divorced, they might as well have been.

Bill will be there all day and most of the night. He will wonder where his wife is, if she still is his wife. He will most likely come home at midnight, drunk from the flask of Four Roses he fills each morning and drains throughout the day. He will crawl into bed, probably next to Sharon, who sometimes will fall asleep in the loveseat so sometimes he has the bed to himself, which he enjoys, and he will pass out and then wake at 4:30 to go back to Division Street.

At the store, the man is hanging tinsel around a door frame. His right hand is battered and bloody. It looks as though he were in a street fight, but there's no way of knowing if this is in fact the case. It's possible he put his fist through a wall during a conversation with

Sharon. It might've had something to do with the puppies from last year and who was responsible for what happened.

It is five days before Christmas and business is going well. On December 26, they will burn the building down. Then they will flee to British Columbia. This is the plan they have in place, though it is subject to change because Sharon hasn't been at the store in days. She hasn't been in the bed when Bill has crawled into it the last few nights. It is possible she has left him or will leave him. It's also possible she's dead. Bill hasn't heard from her.

The woman named Sharon, who is probably still alive, is thinking about leaving her husband and filing for divorce. She has talked it over with some friends, the ins and outs, the implications and consequences. It's unclear if she will ever make up her mind. She is the kind of woman who can consider something for years and never make a decision. The loveseat is a perfect example. She has wanted to either reupholster the loveseat or get a new one for five years. She's discussed both options with her husband, who is indifferent. He has told her to do whatever she wants with the loveseat. This is one small example of why she might leave him someday.

She is not one for violence so she's never considered stabbing her husband while he sleeps. She's never considered drugging him and then smothering him with a pillow.

I can't say that my own mother didn't have these thoughts because I'm sure she did.

This is one reason Sharon hasn't slept next to Bill in days. Last week she hid a butcher knife in the nightstand drawer on her side of the bed. She had no real intention of using it on her husband, but wanted it there in case she changed her mind.

It's possible she leaned over her husband with the knife in her hand and wondered what kind of sound it would make. It's possible she decided it would depend on what part of his body she plunged it into.

The man is down on Division hawking trees.

The man doesn't know where the woman is, either his wife or his ex-wife, Sharon. He is hanging tinsel and she is somewhere else. She is supposed to be helping him. She is supposed to watch the register. There are only five or six people wandering around the store and now the man has to be available to answer questions and cover the register while hanging tinsel at the same time.

It is too much for any man to do, but especially Bill, because just look at him.

The woman is not at home sitting on a loveseat. She does not have her legs folded beneath her. She is not comfortable.

They do not own a loveseat. They considered buying one once but decided they couldn't afford it. They decided they couldn't see themselves sitting in a loveseat.

It is currently snowing in British Columbia. It has been snowing for three hours and will continue for another six. By the time it stops snowing there will be nearly a foot on the ground.

It's possible the woman is in British Columbia and playing in the snow. It's possible she is there by herself, but it's just as possible she is there with another man whose name doesn't matter, but if it does we should call him Alberto, who sounds like he could be Mexican or Puerto Rican.

It's possible they are sharing a woodpecker pie, which is a recipe that has been in Alberto's family for generations. You can use real woodpecker meat, but you don't have to. The Alberto family makes it every year for Christmas.

The man is hanging tinsel in the store and talking to customers. He tells them he opened the store with his wife but that he is a widower now. It's possible he is telling the truth. When he talks to customers he calls her Trina, but he means Sharon. And she might be anywhere in the world, with anyone, doing anything at all.

Buggery

The man next to me has a bug crawling on him and I watch the bug crawl all over the man until I lose track of it. The bug seems to have found a place to nest in a fold of the man's shirt. It looks like a ladybug but it is not a ladybug. The man doesn't know that he has a bug crawling on him or that it seems to have found a place to nest in a fold of his shirt. The man doesn't know that I've been watching and know the whole story. I decide it isn't my place to tell him. I decide that this poor bastard has brought this on himself because he is slovenly, like I'm sometimes accused of being because I keep books stacked up in my house from floor to ceiling. Whenever I am asked about the towers of books I tell people the books are mine and they should buy their own books. If I tell this to the man with the bug he will likely get upset. Time was you could talk to people and not upset them but you can't anymore. Look where all this talking has gotten us, particularly in regards to me and Esperanza. I haven't spoken with her since our dinner downtown a couple of weeks ago, which is a shame because it's possible we are desperately in love with each other. It's also a shame the man next to me is slovenly and has a bug crawling all over him. He is a Chinese man and he is reading a Chinese newspaper. Understand that I am not saying he is slovenly because he is Chinese nor am I saying that all Chinese men are slovenly. But this particular Chinese man is slovenly and how you know this is because he has a bug crawling on him. This would be true of anyone, be they Chinese or from some other godforsaken place. Except for my Sofia, that one time in a lush meadow on her grandfather's estate. We were out for a walk after Tanya had made a spectacle of herself in that sundress she always wore. My Sofia told me I wasn't Tanya's idea of a handsome man when she caught me with my hand on Tanya's posterior. I was nearly inconsolable, though I tried not to show it. If I close my eyes I can still see my Sofia next to me with that colorful butterfly on the side of her head like some kind of perfectly applied bauble, the look on her face one of naked contempt. This is when I wonder if anyone has ever seen a bug crawling on me in the subway. I don't think I could ever allow this to happen, but who can say for sure. Maybe this slovenly Chinese man would've said the same thing. The only difference is he would've said it in Chinese so I wouldn't have been able to understand him. I don't know if he speaks Cantonese or Mandarin and I don't think it makes a difference because I can't understand either.

How to Live, What to Do

At night, over dinner, we look at each other. Someone says please pass the potatoes and we pass that person potatoes. We enjoy our potatoes but never talk about them. They are potatoes. We discuss the day's events, if there were any, if we can remember. Too many of our days are eventless, so most often there is nothing to discuss. We look at each other and eat our potatoes and wait until everyone is finished.

We're certain the weather is the same, as it is still freezing cold. It is always cold now and people say we are at the beginning of the next ice age. Still, the sun continues to rise and set at the appropriate times. There is wind and rain and snow and hail. There are seasons, although the last two summers lasted only two weeks with temperatures reaching no higher than fifty degrees Fahrenheit.

We don't know who we're looking at over dinner, which is why we spend time looking. We think it's important to look.

We still go to work. We have jobs. Crops are tended, but now they are underground. Basic social services, shops, schools have all maintained regular hours on the days they are open, which is twice a week.

The people around the table could be anyone in the world, though this is unlikely. We're pretty sure the people around the world have stayed home and around their own kitchen tables.

Sometimes we think we recognize someone, a grown woman, a young boy, a gesture or expression, a hairstyle.

Everyone has theories, but the theories don't amount to anything, don't explain what's happened. What we know is no one remembers anything anymore. That's all anyone can say with certainty. We try not to talk about it over dinner.

This was also around the same time the drinking water went bad, according to the newspaper I found in the rubble of the old library. It started in one Michigan city and spread from there.

It's not entirely true that no one remembers anything. We can remember certain things, certain functions and responsibilities. For instance, there is a team that handles heating and cooling.

Some of us seem smarter than the rest. Some of us are more assertive.

We tend to listen to the smart and assertive ones.

Most of the men have grown long beards.

The women look tired. They look like they need to go to bed and stay there.

We have meetings where we discuss theories, where we discuss new protocols, how to live, what to do. It is important everyone attends the meetings and for the most part everyone does.

We try to rotate who runs the meetings, meaning who has the gavel and says things like the motion carries and the meeting is adjourned. No one likes this responsibility.

How to Live, What to Do is written on a sign that hangs in the auditorium where we have the meetings. We hand out leaflets with How to Live, What to Do emblazoned across the cover.

Here we have instructions from how to make pancakes to what to do in the event of a fire or mass shooting.

We don't think we had these kinds of meetings before, but we have them now.

Now people go outside into the weather and forget to put on clothes. What you see is women in nightgowns, men in pajamas, walking to the mailbox or putting out the garbage. Some are naked. Whenever we see a naked person we are supposed to bring them a coat and take them inside.

Some people think it's the water again. They think they remember a story about a chemical company upriver, something about PCBs, whatever those are.

Others think it's because of the power lines or the power plant or that it's gotten into the potatoes somehow. We used to hear planes at night, crop dusters, so maybe it was that.

The neighbors seem to remember what's happened, why things are the way they are now, but they're not talking. They never attend the meetings. Sometimes we discuss the neighbors over dinner and at the meetings. We don't know what's wrong with them or what's right or why they won't talk. Whenever we pass them in the halls they hiss. They never look us in the eye.

Part of the problem is we can't remember what the neighbors were like before. We don't recognize them, but we don't recognize ourselves, either.

What we do now is if you can't find your way home by 8 p.m. you can go into any apartment and spend the night. Most people don't sleep in the same place twice in a row, though we're not sure if this is actually true.

What happens is you go into an apartment and say, I'm home. Whoever is there welcomes you as though you are family, which could well be the case. Everyone spends a minute or so hugging and kissing everyone else.

We ask how was your day and we answer the best we can.

Sometimes we pour drinks for each other. We drink everything straight, whiskey, vodka, red wine.

One theory has it that we've been organized into these neighborhoods because we all look like each other. Presumably there are other neighborhoods where the people look like each other but not like us.

According to the mailboxes a lot of us have three names, meaning first names, middle names, and last names. Sometimes the middle name sounds like a last name and it could be a maiden name if such is the case. We think almost everyone here is married, has a family. All of us have agreed to act this way.

There is one apartment, the neighbors', that's marked with a special flag so that everyone knows not to go there. Once in a while some of us forget and are expelled.

Apparently the neighbors do this without rancor.

Every day, at work, someone has us go into one of the rooms with a blackboard and every day there is something new written on it. We take our seats and look at the board. Our seats are the ones you find in most classrooms, with a desk designed for right-handed people. We aren't allowed to speak to each other while we are in the room. We aren't allowed to look at each other, either.

This is why we try to look at each other at the dinner table.

They give us thirty minutes to look at the board. They have us think directly onto the legal pad sitting atop our desks. We think like this for the allotted time and then are dismissed. Most often they shuffle us to a different room with a different board and we have to think about what's written on this one. We never see the other teams shuffling into the rooms we were just in, but we know there are other teams. They tell us how the other teams thought better than us last week. Sometimes they tell us the score, how much we lost by. It's always embarrassing to hear the results.

Some of us think the neighbors are members of the other teams.

In every room there is a sofa pushed against the back wall. We never look at the sofa but they tell us before each session that the body is back there if we want. They say it exactly like that—the body is back there if we want.

They don't say what we might want the body for.

During quiet time, when the lights are off and we rest our heads on the desks, some of us go over to the sofa.

Today the body fell from the sofa and landed on the carpet, but the neighbors couldn't hear that. The body landed softly, like it had been laid down on a soft surface, like it was a baby put to bed.

It's not as if the neighbors don't make noise themselves. Yesterday one of them was trudging back and forth in high-heeled shoes. We listened to the high-heeled shoes and imagined what it would be like to walk in them.

We knocked on the ceiling with a broom handle and they knocked back. The knocking went on for about twenty minutes.

At night, over dinner, we sometimes discuss what goes on at work, if we can remember. We never talk about the body at dinner. They told us this, they said, never talk about the body at dinner or with anyone who is not a colleague. Furthermore, they said, never talk about the body with a colleague, either.

I, myself, have never gone to the back of the room. I do think about it sometimes, though.

As such there is almost nothing to talk about during dinner. This is when we try to play a game of charades or some other group activity. Sometimes it's cards. Sometimes we tell each other stories.

Even if I were to go to the back of the room I'm not sure what I'd do with the body.

One of us starts and begins with something we can't understand, something about coal miners. You aren't supposed to ask questions until after the story is over, so we sit and listen. One of us says, we aren't certain what coal miners do, but we're sure they wake early in the morning to do it.

The person telling the story is a woman of indeterminate age. She has a prominent nose and it does something to her voice. She sounds like a cartoon character. She is wearing a brassiere over her sweater. You see this sometimes. It only looks wrong to some of us. We've been told we shouldn't correct each other unless someone is in danger.

Then she says something about the coal miner's hands. She says they've been through a lot, that they need a rest .

This is what stands for a story now.

Sometimes we let the children go off and play outside because they don't know any better.

The children are never allowed in the meetings.

We were at our window once watching the children in the street. They were having a game of touch football. One of them went out for a pass and kept on going until she was out of sight. For a second we were concerned but then we assumed she would find a place to spend the night. We told the remaining children to come inside so they could get ready for bed.

We told them they played great, that they were all wonderful players. We asked what happened to the one who went out for the long pass and didn't come back. They said she was supposed to run a fly pattern but got confused. Then they said it looked like she went beautiful and they were right.

Because I can remember this sort of thing and recount it people listen to what I say.

I'm certain this helps no one.

Most of us wanted to go back to our own rooms or whatever rooms we would settle on later once the body was on the floor like this, as it was late in the day. Most of us were tired and had to get up tomorrow. Not everyone has to get up for work every day, but everyone said they did. The truth is most of us don't have to report in most days. Some of us stay in our rooms and do God knows what.

Sometimes, over dinner, we discuss what life must've been like before. Some of us blame the coal miners or the police. We think we remember that they used to shoot the citizens in the face or poison the air.

Sometimes the police would choke you to death instead of shooting you in the face. They did this if you called them on the phone for help or sold cigarettes or passed a counterfeit twenty at a convenience store.

Almost all of us talk about going back to our own people, finding them somehow. We're almost sure that we all have our own families. It's not that we don't regard each other as family, as our people, but we think we have other people elsewhere, too, in other apartments.

We wish them well when we can, when we can remember. We raise a glass and say something nice.

When the children go to bed you're left with your spouse for the evening. This is who you go to bed with and who you'll wake up next to in the morning. You are expected to conduct yourself accordingly.

So far we haven't had a problem in this regard.

That night, in bed, I said to the person next to me, it looked like she went beautiful. The person next to me said what is that and I answered it was what the children said about the child who went out for a pass but didn't come back. I said I like the way it sounded. I said it might be the answer to what's happened to everyone. The person next to me didn't know what I was talking about, didn't remember anyone saying anything.

Then we made love.

In the morning, over breakfast, neither of us said anything to each other.

As we were eating breakfast I saw three naked people walking down the street.

We think the ones who don't have to report in are the ones who go to the back of the room with the body. At least, this is one working theory.

It is all very experimental, what goes on at work. It probably makes sense to someone somewhere, like the government.

It was suggested we draw lots to see who would take the body away so this is what we did. The process was equitable and went off without incident. One of us with soft-soled shoes drew the body lot and this signaled the end of the workday.

Everyone was told to be mindful of the neighbors on the way out.

The person who had to take the body away had curly red hair and a beard. I remember someone telling him that red-headed people were being phased out. I remember him looking confused and angry.

He said what does that mean and someone said it has to do with evolution or the government.

Three of us were charged with helping him load the body into a wheelbarrow. All kinds of equipment are kept in the basement at work, including four wheelbarrows.

This is when I stopped the one with the red hair and beard and pulled him aside. We let everyone else file past us. I held his arm and told him to hang on.

After some back and forth I asked him where he was going to take the body. He said he couldn't tell me so I asked him why not. He said he didn't know.

This is when I hit him in the head with a lunchbox. Then I started kicking him until he lost consciousness.

Here's what's interesting, I have no idea why I did this.

I didn't have anything against this man, even though he did have red hair.

I took the wheelbarrow and wheeled it to the other side of town. I didn't know what I was going to do once I'd gotten there, but I thought this was a good place to take the body.

I remember feeling a certain exhilaration as I was wheeling the body away. I remember running very fast. I don't think anyone saw me and even if they did no one would know what to make of it.

I was a blur.

I'm sure it looked like I'd gone beautiful.

It felt better than making love to the last ten or twenty spouses I've had.

When I'd left him the red-headed man was still unconscious. I thought maybe I should try to resuscitate him but I couldn't remember how that was supposed to work.

If anyone asks I will say he was phased out.

I remembered that we had a meeting scheduled for that evening, so that's where I went when I was finished.

I arrived a few minutes late and the meeting was already in session.

We don't call anyone by name at the meetings even though there are names on the mailboxes. We use terms of endearment most of the time, like Sweetheart and Lovely. During this particular meeting someone suggested that we pick out names from the mailboxes and adopt them as our own, that it would be more civilized this way. The person who suggested this said we could wear nametags.

So, what we said was, Sweetheart, we don't think this is a good idea. Someone called out I second the motion and all in favor say aye so almost all of us said aye. There were only one or two naysayers so the motion carried. Then someone banged the gavel and called meeting adjourned so we all stood up and filed out into the hallway where everyone kissed everyone else goodbye.

A Better Class of People

Some snowdrops ask a woman with a baby papoosed to her chest if she'd like to sit down. Two or three of them ask at the same time and she says yes and sits herself down like she is the queen of Manhattan Island. How come they never ask me if I'd like to sit down is what I ask them after her highness sits down with the baby. I was standing right next to this woman and was on the subway for a dozen stops before she even got on. Sometimes it's like I'm invisible to everyone in the world. I tell them this and then I say you can't see what I have papoosed to my chest now can you. I tell them if they knew what was wrong with me they would start a fundraiser or candlelight vigil. This is when I realize that the woman with the baby papoosed to her chest looks like Esperanza, whom I haven't seen in months. By this time the snowdrops have gone back to their own lives and the woman who looks like Esperanza has either fallen asleep or is nursing her baby right in front of everyone. I can't tell what she's doing because I'm trying not to look at her the same way I tried not to look at Esperanza. I tried hard to keep my hands to myself but it wasn't always easy. I'm not saying the woman is Esperanza, but that she looks like her. She has the same hair and eyes and skin and bumps. One reason I don't think it's Esperanza is because she wouldn't betray me and have someone else's baby, not even with her new husband. Meanwhile I'm still standing up and trying to balance myself because I don't want to touch the pole or the bars or straps. They did a study once on the germs people leave on the subway poles and you wouldn't believe it. This is only one reason people should offer me a seat on the subway, but they never do. I can tell they think they're a better class of people and maybe they're right. The truth is whenever I am sitting down I don't get up for anyone, no matter who they are or what they have strapped to their chests.

Which One's Will

I could hear choking and laughing but couldn't tell who was choking and who was laughing. There were about ten of us altogether, on either side of the room, all spread out. I wasn't the one choking, but I do choke more than I should. My problem is whenever I think about swallowing food I choke instead. I'm not sure if this happens to other people.

It's when I have too much in my mouth that I start to choke and sometimes I have to reach in with my fingers to keep myself from passing out. Only once or twice has someone had to get behind me and do the maneuver.

I'm not sure which one was choking this time. It's not unusual for someone to start choking during mealtime. It's the bread they serve and how dry it is. You'd think they want us to choke and you'd be right.

I remember hearing the stories growing up. This great-grandfather choked on a chicken bone, that cousin choked on his own birthday cake and so on. It's the same way with the breathing. I am out walking and everything is fine. I might be on my way to the store or to the park or God knows where as it's not important. What is important is that I am out and about and walking and not thinking about anything in particular. But then I start to think about my breathing and I forget how. I collapse right there on the street.

We are supposed to practice chewing and breathing every day. They instruct us to take a bite of our lunch and then chew it at least twenty times. We are to swallow it slowly on its own, without the aid of water to help it down. We are to breathe in through our nose and out through our mouth as we swallow. There is a pitcher of water in the middle of the table but we aren't allowed to drink from it. There are glasses in front of our places at the table but they are empty. This is why so many of us choke here during mealtime and it's me as often as anyone.

My chest hurts and my vision blurs and my mouth goes dry and then I'm down. Only sometimes do I get the shakes. I know some people think I shake all the time but it's not true. People are always careful to step around me whenever I do get the shakes, though. People are good this way.

I never look them in the eye when they step around me because I am usually convulsing and can't keep my eyes open. Still, I know they're there and I know they are making an effort to step around me convulsing on the pavement.

I don't know the others all spread out in the room here. They don't let us talk to each other and we don't wear nametags. They don't let us look at each other, either, so the nametags wouldn't help. Once I tried to look up while I was in the middle of chewing and felt a lash across my back.

We have all been selected to live here. I heard one of the guards call us detainees, but I'm not sure that's true. I don't think I feel detained.

I never swallow my tongue and only once or twice has someone stuck fingers in my mouth to keep me from doing it.

If I had to guess about the people all spread out here I wouldn't.

If you were to ask someone else they might say they are all hard-luck cases like me, that we are members of the troubled class.

I was made to drop out of school early on. I think I almost finished one of the middle grades, but that was as far as it went.

Even still, I accomplished great things before I was sent here.

I assume they are all men, too, the people surrounding me here. I don't know why I assume this. It seems wrong if one of these people were a woman.

I'm sure women have their own facilities elsewhere.

What makes this day noteworthy is the one I heard choking wound up choking to death.

Doubtless the ones laughing were the supervisors. They are heartless and sadistic meaning they are regular people like you can find anywhere.

Who I wouldn't thank are those who do not step around. Sometimes people kick me when I'm flopping around on the pavement. Sometimes after they kick me they rifle through my pockets and steal my wallet. The kicks almost always hurt but sometimes it's like they are jumpstarting the breathing.

I do like women, but I'm glad they're not here, if the other ones spread out in the room aren't them, which I assume they're not.

What I like about women is how they look and feel. I sometimes like how they sound if they have a nice voice, which is usually a fifty-fifty proposition.

I'm not saying I like all women. There was one named Trina who abused me and I wasn't crazy about Django, either.

I almost never fight back because it's pointless. You can't have an attack and fight back at the same time.

You can't smell the food because it is odorless. I think they do this on purpose. The food is also tasteless, therefore it is impossible to enjoy, which is probably the point.

We are allowed out every other week and it's nice. We are free to act like normal people and go into shops and stores. We can stand in traffic should we care to do so. I only stand in traffic when I feel like it or when I have to go protest.

I know that I'm making history when I stand in traffic. I know that one day millions will join me and maybe then things will change.

We are allowed to see the picture show if one is playing. It's true we are supervised during these outings, but the supervisors are instructed not to interfere with our behaviors.

It was only a day or two after I'd arrived here that they gave me the electric shock treatments. I can't say that it was altogether unpleasant. I may've even had an orgasm.

I have only seen the one picture show. I couldn't tell who was at war but both sides meant business. There was a battery or battalion dug in and another marching toward them. They were spread out on opposite sides of a trench. A commander went up and down the line and told everyone to hold their fire. He told them to reload and then he gave them the final command. Fire at will, he said. This is when I yelled out, which one's Will, but no one laughed or admonished me.

Time was you could joke with people and grab their round parts and everyone understood it was all in good fun.

We are part of a team but we aren't teammates. They are keeping tabs on us and how we chew our food and swallow it. It is okay if one of us dies because that means they will learn something. I think it's probably an honor to take part in this. I think maybe we should count ourselves lucky.

They will probably keep this study going until all of us die.

After lunch they put us in our own rooms to do what we will. I've never been in anyone else's room so when I'm in mine doing what I will I assume they are in theirs doing likewise.

I haven't come close to dying, I don't think.

I thought maybe they would let us go after that first one died, but they didn't.

I never think about leaving because I don't think it's possible.

I also think where would I go and the answer is nowhere.

Sometimes people would step softly around me and other times they would have at me like it was open season.

We aren't allowed to ask questions and even if we were I wouldn't know what to ask.

My name isn't Will, in case you were wondering.

I'm not going to say what my name is because I don't want to be held responsible and because I can't remember.

I don't think anyone has called me by my name for too many years.

So, it's better to think of me as the one who was choking but not laughing.

At the same time think of me as the one leading the revolution.

Better still, think of me as the one on the pavement and maybe I'm shaking and convulsing at the same time.

It's up to you whether or not you step softly around.

The Future Home of the Wymans

I'm sorry I joked about hanging your grandmother is what the young woman next to me said to the young woman next to her. I don't know where they were going but I was on the way to see my new doctor who might refer me to someone who performs kidney transplants on an outpatient basis. But the bigger problem is I have trouble sleeping if I'm not in my own bed. I don't know why but I can never fall asleep or stay asleep when I try it in some other bed. But also it's my kidneys. They don't work anymore. My old doctor wanted to put me on dialysis, but I don't want to walk around with anything sticking into me or running out of me. He also wanted to repair my hernia and give me a prostate exam, but I never let him down there. I also have a gluten sensitivity and peanut allergy but there's nothing they can do for that. Life is unbearable for me is what I'm saying, but I'm not alone because nearly seventy-five percent of all citizens are now sensitive to gluten and allergic to peanuts. But I'm more concerned with getting a good night's sleep than I am with my kidneys. It's always been this way, from the time I lived with my own grandmother right next door to the future home of the Wymans. My grandmother didn't know what to do with me, which I never blamed her for. I've never known what to do with myself, either. We never met the Wymans, but they were building a home next door that had a sign out front saying The Future Home of the Wymans. My grandmother sent me over there every night to see if the construction workers left anything behind. This is the woman who more or less raised me and taught me right from left and the difference between scotch and bourbon. She also taught me how to fall asleep at night if you didn't have enough scotch or bourbon on hand. It had to do with relaxing each part of your body in a particular order. This technique never worked for me. I think about telling this to the young woman sitting next to me but decide against it. She doesn't need to know how I can't fall asleep at night or how the Wymans never seemed to move into the future with everyone else. It's possible that these two young women are sisters and their parents are the Wymans or it's possible that they're lifelong friends and have never even heard of the Wymans. These two aren't Tanya and my Sofia, that much I know. But whenever I see two women together that might be sisters I can't help but think of Tanya and my Sofia. Either way, these two on the subway have been in cahoots since they were little girls in pigtails, playing ring around the rosie or whatever little girls do. This is how they can joke about each other's grandmothers. My own grandmother didn't let me associate with little girls because she said they were the devil's playthings. So I don't know what little girls do now or what they did back then. I also don't know what happened to my grandmother. I don't think she ever hanged herself but I don't stay up nights thinking about it. By now we are close to my stop so I decide to tell all of this to the young woman next to me but she doesn't respond. Instead she makes a face to her friend and they both laugh like everyone is in on the same grandmother joke. This is when I lift my shirt up to show her the scar from my last transplant surgery, when they switched out my own liver for a better one. I tell them this is one part I can never get to relax which is why I can't sleep at night and they both answer by telling me to keep my pants on. This is when I start laughing because I never intended to lower my pants in the first place, at least until the doctor's office and probably not even then.

Decisions

I've been making decisions since I woke up this morning but it's not a problem. Nothing I decide will make a difference to anyone. When I say anyone I mean my family and friends, if I still have any. The last time I tried to think of someone who might still be a friend I couldn't. I don't talk to anyone in my family anymore, either, and that includes both my mother and brother. I also mean my neighbors and the people in town when I say that it won't make a difference to anyone. I don't know any of my neighbors by name, but I know the decisions I make won't affect them.

The biggest decision I've made is that I'm moving, but I don't know where yet. I don't have a car anymore so wherever I move to I have to get there by train or bus. I won't make that decision until it comes time to do so. I imagine it will depend on where I'm going and if it's a train or a bus that goes there. I can't say that I prefer one method of transportation to the other. It's all the same since I don't have a car anymore.

My brother is the one who stole my car, which is why I stopped talking to him. Actually, he wound up going through the windshield of that car when I was driving him to the hospital one night. He got himself beaten up due to a rumor I'd started, something about his heritage and sexuality. He wound up in a coma from which he never recovered, but that's life for you. Sometimes you go through a windshield and wind up in a coma and sometimes you end up like me. I'm not sure which is worse and I'm not sure it makes a difference.

Regardless, I won't talk about why I don't talk to my mother anymore.

My mother doesn't know the first thing I decided this morning was if I wanted to get out of bed and the answer was no. So I went back to sleep for another hour but woke up when I heard the doorbell ring. I decided I didn't want to answer the doorbell so I decided to let it keep ringing. The person who was ringing the doorbell kept ringing it for a solid minute. I'm sure it wasn't my mother or brother because neither of them knows where I live. Also, my brother is dead now, I think.

I'm not sure anyone knows where I live except for my landlord who won't be my landlord come tomorrow morning.

I decided tomorrow is when I'm going to move somewhere else. I stopped paying rent six months ago and have been getting letters shoved under my door ever since. They say I have to pay rent, that I have to pay late fees for missing last month's payment and the month before that. I haven't answered the letters because why would I. It's possible the landlord has turned me in, as you can get turned in for anything these days. Someone tried to turn me in once because I'm half Puerto Rican. The funny thing is it was a Mexican who tried this, someone I used to work with, a pendejo named Jorge.

Starting tomorrow I'm on the road bound for anywhere other than Mexico or Puerto Rico and so I no longer feel any obligations. Maybe it was the landlord ringing the doorbell this morning. When I say ringing the doorbell I mean knocking on the door. I don't have a doorbell and never have. I don't know why I said I did other than I like the sound of it better. It's more civilized. I was thinking about this when I decided to let the person at the door keep knocking on it. I thought this would be a better experience if it were a doorbell. I wondered what it would take to get a doorbell installed but I knew my landlord would never do it. The landlord is a criminal from some godforsaken country no one has ever heard of, which is why I stopped paying rent six months ago.

A rat bit my mother while she was trying to fix a leaking pipe under the kitchen sink. Everyone knows it's the super's job to do things like this but we haven't had a super since the last one quit two years ago. The last super was from Europe and the one before that was from South America and they were both worthless. I'm not saying that everyone from Europe and South America is worthless but if you said it I wouldn't argue.

I also wouldn't argue against everyone from North America and Asia being worthless, too.

I think the supers were deported and this is why we don't have one anymore. I'd mentioned this to my mother who said she could come over to fix the leak. I told her I didn't think it was a good idea but she didn't care. This was when the rat bit her and we had to call an exterminator who charged four hundred dollars. I told them there was a rat and my mother trapped it in the bathroom. I was in the living room watching television at the time. I like to scan the channels for something better, which tells you all you need to know about me. I heard her scream and run into the kitchen, which was when she told me about the rat. She told me other things, too, but that's between the two of us. I decided to take my mother outside on the stoop to calm her down. This is when I walked across the street to the bodega for a big can of beer. My mother has always liked to drink big cans of beer and so I thought this would be a good time for one. I brought it back to her wrapped inside a brown paper bag and told her to drink it. I told her let's not make a big deal out of this, but I won't repeat what she said to that.

When I say the rat bit her I'm saying that only for the landlord's benefit. The truth is the rat didn't bite my mother, but it did brush past her and this is the kind of thing that can shock someone into an early grave, particularly if they are old and enfeebled like my mother. I was worried for her health, but she started to feel better after a few slugs of beer.

I decided then and there I wouldn't pay rent ever again and that it would serve the landlord right.

I knew I couldn't go back to sleep at this point so this is when I decided I was up for good. I decided to get out of bed and go into the bathroom. I did what I do every morning in the bathroom but decided I wasn't going to shower because I'd showered last night. I don't always shower at night but sometimes I have to because I get home late and it is hot out and I sweat through my clothes. I almost always sweat through my clothes when it's hot and this is why I decide to stay inside for most of the summer if I can help it. I don't like the feeling of sweating through my clothes and I don't think anyone else does, either. My mother and brother used to make fun of me for sweating through my clothes, but that's not one of the reasons I don't talk to them anymore. I probably won't talk to either of them ever again and it serves everybody right.

I do know that I want to move someplace where I won't have to sweat as much. I think that might be the most important factor when I decide where I'll move to and how I might get there.

What Is or Isn't Collapsing

Four Deaf kids are talking shit about me on the other side of the car. I can tell it's me they're talking about because every so often they look my way and start in with the hands and fingers. I'm wearing headphones so they probably think I'm showing off. There are maybe ten people with headphones in so I don't know why they have singled me out. I tried smiling at the girl, but I think she took it the wrong way. Something in her face told me I should fuck off because she doesn't take kindly to older men who smile at her on the subway with only one thing on their mind. I'm not sure why she thinks this about me because it's not the truth. I almost want to tell them about my tinnitus, that I have it in both ears now and it's awful. I could tell them that I'm losing my hearing, too, particularly in my left ear, and I'm too old to learn sign language. I could never go on a subway and talk to anyone after I'm deaf, so these kids don't know how lucky they are. They're all spread out in the car, occupying different benches, and still they can talk to each other and not bother anyone. This is probably the greatest gift but instead they go around in pity for themselves. I don't talk to anyone on the subway if I can help it and I almost never take the subway with someone I know. And the girl I smiled at, it had nothing to do with what's spilling out of the top of her blouse. So, it's something like a Mexican standoff, except that would have to involve another person so it's not exactly like that, either. Maybe if there was a blind person in this subway car, one with a seeing-eye dog and a cane, then we could have a real Mexican standoff. And if everyone had their guns on them we could all shoot each other in the face. That would be glorious. You do see people shooting other people on the subway so it's not impossible, but I should stop thinking about it because thinking gets you nowhere. Instead I could tell them I'm going deaf on account of the tinnitus and blind because of keratoconus, which I've had for thirty years now. I can try telling them this. I can try schooling them, but what then. These kids don't want to hear from the likes of me and maybe they're right. The song I'm listening to with my headphones has some poor bastard asking to borrow lungs because his are collapsing. He says that Jesus was an only son and love his only concept, but it all goes to hell when strangers come in foreign tongues and dirty up the doorstep. This proves that even Jesus didn't like Europeans and South Americans. You can't blame Jesus because it was the Europeans that killed him and the South Americans stood by and did nothing to stop it. So when I look at these kids I see the Romans and Incas in league with each other and you know it doesn't even occur to them that I might be Jesus on the cross in this scenario.

Eviction Notice

Someone will have to testify, the man says to me, out loud and in front of people I don't know. I don't know why he is talking to me and I don't know who has to testify about what. The man has two dogs resting at his feet. The dogs look like cousins once removed. The man looks like he shouldn't have any dogs, let alone two that look like this. I tell him I have my own problems. I tell him he should be ashamed of himself. He says, someone will have to leave an historical record to be found in a cave underneath rubble and sediment.

I don't know this man. I don't know what he does, where he comes from. He is across from me on the front porch of someone's house. I don't think the house is his. I'm not sure if you're supposed to have dogs on the front porch of someone else's house, unless maybe they are in service to someone or something or if you know the homeowner personally. I can't tell if this man is in need of service, if he is blind. He is wearing sunglasses but that means nothing. From what I can see he is in need of a new wardrobe, something suitable for civilized people.

I'm not sure whose house it is.

I'm not sure who the other people are, either. Some of them are men, others women. They all look like people you can find anywhere, doing anything. I decide I don't need to know anything about any of them.

The one thing I do know about people is they don't want you to bleed all over their things. This I learned from my mother. When I was a kid she would beat me with a cheese grater and then tell me not to bleed all over the floor. I always tried my best not to bleed for her. Sometimes, when I was able to staunch the bleeding, I would ask if she was proud of me. She almost always answered yes.

Why I'm thinking of this is because I sliced my finger open while making breakfast and I'm still bleeding.

I see the man with the two dogs looking at me, trying to decide if he should say something else, make some sort of effort. Then he looks at a guitar leaning against the rail to my right. It's missing a string and seems as if it got run over by a truck once or twice.

Perhaps he knows me, this man with the two dogs. Perhaps he thinks I am his brother or a coworker.

Let those who find it point fingers and mock, he says, like they can do better.

I am on my way home but I stopped here when someone called me by name and offered me a drink. I think the person who did this is a friend of mine, as I seem to recognize him, though I don't recognize the house. I'm assuming the man with the dogs is a friend of a friend, one I've never met before. Or it's possible they were all friends of my mother. They seem familiar in the kind of way that doesn't mean anything to anyone.

The man with the two dogs says, it looks like you're bleeding.

I say, I'm a person, too.

I don't know who this guitar belongs to but I assume it's the homeowner. This is why I can pick it up and start playing, because I was invited. I was told I should make myself at home, that I should make myself comfortable. I haven't been comfortable in years, not even in my own apartment, which has never seemed like home to me. I think maybe it's because I don't have any furniture and the floors aren't hardwood. There's this linoleum covering the floors and it's terrible. I mop it every night for an hour or two but it never comes clean.

Instead of furniture I have towers of books, which I've fashioned in such a manner that they make hallways. The inside of my apartment is a maze. I get lost every so often, but eventually I find where it is I have to go, which is the kitchen or bathroom. Only once I couldn't find my way to the kitchen or bathroom but I don't like to think about that day.

No one comes over anymore and my life is better because of it. What I do instead of people is I sit on the floor and watch the television, though it seems to be breaking down. The picture cuts in and out, as does the sound.

No one pays any attention to me as I play. Everyone keeps talking about the great things they are doing or how awful everything is. Meanwhile, I'm making music, even though I've never played guitar before.

The first song I play is a take on some Bach cello concertos. Then I transition into Oye Como Va, which I sing in Spanish.

The lyrics to Oye Como Va is the only Spanish I know, which is why I recite it whenever I talk to anyone from Mexico or Guatemala.

This is when the Mexicans or Guatemalans curse me.

I decide I don't care who might be paying attention because I'm about to be evicted. They've been hanging notices on my door for months now.

I stopped paying rent last year.

I almost tell this to the man across from me but decide against it.

He doesn't need to know about the rat that almost bit my mother and how my life hasn't been the same ever since.

One of the dogs is lying down with one of his front legs folded underneath him. It looks like he couldn't care less about anything or anyone. The other dog moves from one person to another like a beggar, like he is panhandling for food or affection.

I feel a trail of blood running down my finger and wipe it with a handkerchief. Some of it leaks onto the guitar. I look around to see if anyone notices.

I decide not to clean it off yet because I like how it looks, the drops of blood on the body and fretboard. Still, I don't want to have to explain my blood and how it got all over the guitar. When I was a kid I would try to explain myself to my mother and this is when she would beat me with the cheese grater or meat tenderizer. What she beat me with depended on what we were having for dinner that night.

The man says, then the trees with their leaves on inside out, people streaming inland, moving in herds.

I decide not to respond to this because I'm not fluent in this language.

This is when I put down the guitar and walk inside the house to find a bathroom for gauze or a band-aid. There are people inside the house, too, talking to each other and drinking beer. I try not to listen to any of them as I walk down a hallway and through a kitchen, though I overhear someone say, when I look at my shadow my hair looks sad. I don't understand what this means, but I find the bathroom without having to ask anyone for directions and without overhearing anything else.

I open the medicine cabinet and then open and close some drawers. By this time blood is dripping onto the floor. This was something my mother would've beaten me half to death over. It was one thing to spill blood onto the floor, but she hated for me to drip like this.

I don't notice anything about the bathroom floor other than my blood all over it. I can't say if it is linoleum or real tile. This is when someone starts knocking. I say, it's occupied and they say, I'm sorry. I find a roll of paper towels and I tear strips of the paper towel and wrap them around my finger. Next I find a roll of scotch tape and tape the strips around my finger. I don't know if this will stop the bleeding, but at least I've made an effort.

I go back outside, pick up the guitar, play a gypsy jazz song like Django Reinhardt. The man with the dogs is still there, but he's not listening to me.

I'm not sure where I'll go if they finally throw me out. I can't go back to my mother because I don't know where she is. We lost track of one another years ago, right after she took up with that widower from down south.

So far all they've done is hang notices on my door. If they break in and move all of my stuff outside then I will have to make a decision. It's quite possible I might do something that'll land me on the evening news. It's possible I might decide to shoot this man in the face and take his dogs and go wandering all over the country.

This time tomorrow I might be huddled under an overpass, these two dogs my only reasons for living. A man could do worse, but not by much.

Someone else tries to talk to me, one of the other people, a woman. People are drawn to talent so I'm not surprised. It sounds like I've been playing guitar all my life and do it for a living. I tell her to leave me alone so I can make my music. She says, is that what it is. Then I watch her walk across the porch to bother someone else.

The man with the two dogs laughs. I tell him I'm taking requests.

Maybe we are coworkers or maybe he is one of the brothers I don't know anything about. I remember the brother I did know but I lost track of him when he was in the hospital and they were about to pull the plug for him. I can't remember if our mother beat him like she did me or if she was his mother at all, but I think I remember him liking dogs, even keeping one or two of them as pets.

The man says, a soft rain makes music when it bathes the earth. I tell him I know. I tell him I like to hear it when I sleep.

The Question as We Understand It

The man is telling the woman to shut the fuck up. He tells her this and he tells her this. He is adamant. He is emotional. We don't know what this woman is saying to the man or what she is trying to say. The woman probably wants to go to dinner but the man has already eaten is our best guess. Otherwise, she is complaining about what he does wrong around the house. She seems like someone that likes to go to dinner and keeps house a certain way and he seems like someone who's already eaten and doesn't care about the house. They are standing on the platform waiting for the subway. It is important to the man that the woman shut the fuck up and although we don't know anything about this woman or what she is trying to say we tend to agree with the man in this particular case. We always want quiet, so today we'd prefer it if the woman did, in fact, shut the fuck up. We think she should consider his feelings and needs and though she couldn't possibly know this, we too aren't the best housekeepers and finished dinner less than an hour ago.

Bloodlines

She said there's no such thing as bad weather. I was across the table trying to work up enthusiasm for a turkey sandwich. The sun was in and out and I could feel it doing a number on my head. At the same time I was watching one squirrel chase another and cursing the day I was born.

I considered this about the weather and agreed on the face of it. I always try to be agreeable if all else is equal, which it almost never is. I told her this, too, that I agreed, that there's no such thing as bad weather, but the weather this past year has been awful and everyone knows it.

People say the climate is changing and we are responsible, that we have polluted the world past the point of rescue. This is why there are all these storms killing all these people.

I tried to remember if I had a hat or bandana in the car. Someone somewhere had a hat or bandana, because the sun was up there doing numbers and you can get cancer and die if you're not careful. You can get cancer and die if you are careful, too, but that's this rotten world for you.

She's always been like this, this woman eating a salad, about the weather, about what's good and bad, for as long as I've known her, which is about a month now.

Then she said, I don't understand people like you. I figured this sort of declaration was coming. At the same time the squirrel doing the chasing got distracted and went home.

I took a bite of the sandwich and pretended it took a long time to chew. I pretended I was thinking. I looked out toward the horizon. There was nothing to see there and the nothingness went on for miles, to the edge of the earth.

Everyone knows this about the horizon, but it's always surprising to me.

All during the drive I had to force myself to keep my eyes on the road in front of me. I figured turning my head could only lead to more disappointment.

We were on our way to her people, the ones who'd been wiped out by a series of tornadoes.

What I'm saying is I think I was as close to happy as I could possibly get.

I have trouble with my hearing, but I also have trouble listening. The two aren't necessarily related. She's reeled off a series of names during our monthlong conversation but I'm not sure if they are relations or ex-husbands. They could be the people we are coming to bury or tend to, although she seems like the sort who has made marriage a habit.

It probably wouldn't surprise anyone that I've spent time overseas and behind bars, least of all this woman. People who understand weather know things about the world and the people in it and don't need details. I'm sure she's divorced men with similar backstories and she would be bored if I tried to tell her mine.

It's not impossible that she's done time, too, but I won't ask.

I like her well enough and the upshot is I'd like for her to say something nice about me when we don't know each other anymore.

I eat my sandwich and try not to look at her. I know she wants me to, wants something that resembles an answer, but sometimes you can't look at anything beautiful, let alone answer questions.

This woman is the only person I've ever been able to pick up off the floor and carry somewhere else. What I'm saying is I feel like a giant next to her.

I usually go for sturdier women as I appreciate curves and substance.

Even though some people consider me a midget because I'm only five foot five.

I said that I don't understand me, either. I said there's no use trying. I said the best we can do is hope for the best.

I thought of pointing out the squirrels, how they seem content to chase each other around and eat nuts. I could've talked about instincts, primal needs, and necessities. I could've held them up as models, but the squirrels were gone and not likely to come back.

I'd hoped that we'd see a tornado on our drive but it didn't happen. I kept the radio on in the car, looked to the empty horizon on all sides. I thought I saw a funnel cloud churning towards us once, but it was a swarm of insects.

She said you'll never find one that way. She said what kind of person wants to see a tornado anyway.

I told her they were awful and awesome in equal measure. I talked about the wonders of the natural world.

She said that's because you've never been in one.

The woman and I were somewhere in the middle of the country. The flatlands, the badlands, the this land is your land.

There'd been a series of storms that wiped out a series of peoples.

I told her the earth was defending itself and she looked at me like a dead china doll.

A month ago we were back at the retreat trying to get well. We'd found each other by the pool and I said something about drowning in the shallow end. She said something like it takes one to know one and the next morning I was brushing my teeth with her toothbrush. Later that day we saw it all on the news, the storms and the hucksters covering it.

So I don't know if we're down here to help her family or bury them. She didn't talk much on the ride, didn't say if we were on our way to parents or brothers and sisters, which was fine because I think maybe I'm going deaf, particularly in my right ear. There's a buzzing in there that doesn't go away. I think maybe it's congenital, which means I caught it from my parents who caught it from theirs. Life isn't easy when your bloodline is defective.

I figured I should say something about this particular tragedy, something that could be taken as empathetic or profound. I told her that anything is possible, that her folks might be fine. I said it's possible they lost telephone service but they could be holed up safe and sound in a high school gymnasium.

This is when she said there was no such thing as bad weather because that's how she sees it, like all the snowdrops who want to save the earth.

I almost said the earth doesn't need saving, that it'll be just fine. I wanted to tell her that the people are doomed and that was going to be fine, too, that we weren't meant to live like this anyway.

I imagine we are going to pay respects, dig for survivors, hand out bottled water.

She was the one who suggested we pull over, said she was hungry. She wanted to stretch her legs, get something cold to drink. We were still a hundred miles from where we were going, but it was a good time to stop.

She ran into a relation at the market, some kind of second cousin partially removed. This cousin didn't know anything about the tornadoes, was from another side of the family.

I was introduced as the boyfriend and told it was good of me to do this. I said there was nothing to it and wandered off.

My father used to tell me I was a do-gooder, which wasn't ever true. At least that's what I think he said. I couldn't understand him because he kept his voice down in the back part of his throat behind a swollen tongue and yellow teeth.

I guess I'm the same way, which is why I went to that retreat in the first place. People were there for all sorts of reasons but I was trying to get sober and stay that way. I never told Diana this, that's her name, Diana, the woman I've been referring to. I'm not sure why I didn't refer to her by name before. I didn't want to call her out like that, but she knows who she is and so far I haven't broken any confidences.

I think Diana was hoping to find some part of herself that must've gone missing, some part she needed going forward.

I think my father meant that my heart was usually in the right place, somewhere in the middle of my chest but slightly off-center. But I think it's never been exactly like that, either. I think I've always wanted people to think that about me, but the truth is I couldn't care less nine times out of ten.

When she said I don't understand people like you I believe it was in reference to my position on life and death, the earth and the people debasing it, which is something I thought profound. She accused me of being arch or flippant. Then she asked me why I was driving with her all this way, that it didn't make sense. I thought about explaining myself, but figured it was useless.

When she came back she threw a bandana at me, told me I'd get a sunburn if I didn't cover up.

I imagine pulling into the town in about three hours and being redirected by local officials to certain designated areas. She'll tell the officials that her family lives here and we need to find them, that she hasn't spoken with them in days, that the man driving is her boyfriend and he's here to help, but I'm sure they'll take one look at me and not believe any of it.

What the Living Emit

She wants to know what's my problem and how long I've had it. I ask her to be more specific. I ask her to come on now. She says I know damn well what she's talking about but I don't and it's not even close. When she says I know damn well what she's talking about she makes a gesture with her hands like she's holding a drumstick and hitting a cymbal. I don't think this woman is a drummer so I don't know why she is making this gesture. I don't think I know any drummers and I'm fine with this because I don't like drummers. Drummers go around thinking they're real musicians but everyone knows they're wrong, unless they can play another instrument like guitar or banjo. I always laugh when someone tells me they're a musician and it turns out they're a drummer. I'm looking at the woman drumming in the air like she's hitting a cymbal and I feel sorry for her. This woman has no lips, either. Maybe she has lips, but they are thin and chapped and she hasn't stopped talking since I've known her, which is going on four hours now. I can't remember what started the conversation or why it's still happening. I think maybe I asked her for directions because I'm not at my usual stop. If I were at my usual stop I wouldn't need directions. It's possible I was on my way to an appointment. I almost never leave the house unless I have an appointment and I'm certain today was no exception. What happened was I decided to ask this woman for directions because this wasn't my usual stop and here we are hours later and she wants to know what's my problem and how long I've had it. I'm not sure it's truly been hours but it feels that way. I'm also sure that by now I've missed my appointment and I'll have to reschedule. I can't remember what this particular appointment was for, as I book about a dozen appointments a week. Sometimes I show up to an appointment and they have to remind me why I'm there. Sometimes I expect a kidney transplant but it turns out I'm interviewing for a job. But I miss appointments, too, because I get lost or sidetracked by someone I've asked for directions, like this woman who thinks she's a drummer. The sound of her talking makes me want to go home and cancel the rest of my appointments for the next two weeks. Otherwise, it makes me want to die, I can't decide. I'm sure when I'm dead I won't have to miss appointments and the people I ask for directions will point me the right way. Maybe it's not the sound of her talking that makes me want to go home or die, but rather that she has no lips. I myself have pillow lips, at least that's what Esperanza called them. She said the rest of me was no great shakes but I had a beautiful mouth. I'm no different from most people in that I was wounded. I, too, am alive and on the planet and have appointments and I see people and they say awful things about me and sometimes I want to go home and die. Maybe this is the problem she was talking about earlier or maybe it was because I said something about her lips. I may've asked her what happened to them and did it hurt. Maybe she took offense. It's also possible I was married to this person once. I remember being married to a woman who had no lips. I think maybe that's why we divorced, too. Both the marriage and divorce were mistakes, but it doesn't matter anymore, not today, not now. I can't remember if the woman I was married to was born with no lips or if something happened to her, some kind of accident or catastrophe. Had something happened I'm sure I stood by her for as long as I could stand. I try to be a good person and maybe that's why I'm still talking to this woman even though she's made me miss my appointment and I want to go home and die. She does remind me of my former wife in this respect. The only difference is the woman I was married to played a mean clarinet and wasn't a drummer like this one here.

The Natural Use of the Woman

I began as a child, an infant. I was born.

My father was a natural-born lover's man, like myself. He started before I did because that's what God intended, according to him, my father. He said it was part of a divine plan. My father invoked the divine almost every day and always ended the invocation by looking straight at you as if to say don't even think it.

He probably didn't realize he would spawn someone who would talk this way in front of everyone.

The man had no sense of timing his whole life through. For instance, it might've been better if instead of him bearing me I bore him.

The father is child of the man or however that is supposed to go.

I have always had a hard time with how things should go and at what speed. I always find myself rushing home and then I have nothing to do. I sit on the sofa and wait for inspiration. I don't listen to music, watch television, or read. I don't think about the people I know or the things I've done.

I always find myself rushing through dinner, too, and when I'm finished I have nothing to do again.

I don't know why but I think it's my father's fault. I think I remember my father eating this way and I probably wanted to compete with him so for this I blame my father. In all other respects the man is blameless.

I never saw him dance because he said it was beneath him. He said there was no way to dance and be dignified at the same time.

I never saw him alone because he was always beside himself.

He never talked about his parents, who came here from the island almost a century ago.

Sometimes I have no idea what goes with what. If this shirt goes with these pants, those shoes with that outfit, head with body, person with person, genitals with other genitals. Sometimes it takes hours to get myself dressed.

I don't think I get this from my father, as all I can ever remember him wearing is that one black suit, white button-down, skinny tie, walking shoes.

He was a rolling stone who never strayed from the natural use of the woman, at least that's what he told me. He never said what that meant exactly, but I always liked the sound of it.

Every time I look at a woman I think what can I use this one for, what's natural here.

Most of the time I'm stumped.

I know they feel the same way when they look at me, so no one is disappointed.

I thought to use Betty as a conduit to someone for sexual intercourse and we were supposed to meet for coffee once to do just that as a case in point. However, we never did meet for coffee.

I have no idea why she wanted to meet with me or why anyone would.

I had lunch with my father only once. It was a hotel restaurant somewhere in the American South. They served us pan-seared whatnots in a whosoever sauce. I think it was quite good but I can't remember. The waitress was from Alabama and didn't apologize.

He told me he didn't understand what was happening in the world. He referenced faraway places and people, he talked about Muslims and their women, in hijabs and burkas. He talked about men burning in their lust for one another here at home. He railed against the philistines and sodomites. He talked about how everyone was gluten free range and organic, artisanal and hypoallergenic. These snowdrops, he said, are all pussyfooting do-gooders. I think he implicated me in this, but I can't be sure.

He talked about states in the middle of the country, where they've outlawed these behaviors and begun rounding up the perpetrators.

He said they had the right idea.

He said he was afraid to leave his house, cross the street, until everyone who should be was behind bars or in mass graves.

I told him he should look both ways, that he should glance leftward and rightward and then left again to make sure. I told him if he sees someone on the ground convulsing he should step softly around. He told me he didn't understand what I was talking about.

He told me he never understood me, the things I did, certain behaviors.

Some of these included substances and dress and comportment and those I consorted amongst or around.

He said I was part of the problem and I told him if you're not part of the problem then you're part of the solution.

If he'd asked I would've told him there's no shame in anything anymore. I'd tell him this is America.

I was in the middle of yet another drama with several people over who wanted to spend what kind of time and with whom. I always get myself mixed up with people that make things more complicated than they need to be. They say things like why don't you love me anymore. I say things like I'm sure you don't want an actual list.

I think this is why my father tried hard to have a sit-down with God or one of his minions. My father wanted answers, assurances.

My father said everything changed after God found him.

I never asked why it was that God found him and not the other way around.

I always imagined God walking through deserts and climbing mountains and navigating oceans looking for my father.

My father spoke often of the family line, the family name. He said it was important to keep the bloodlines flowing. He said it was important to plant roots.

I told him I wasn't that sort of bloke, that I was an anti-natalist. I told him that the human race has gone far enough, it's time for something else.

I said never to have been born is best.

He called that blasphemy, said my soul was imperiled. I told him he should see my kidneys.

I said if the bloodlines were important then how come I know nothing about your parents. How come we don't speak the language.

He told me we were Americans and so history is unimportant. He said we are all about the future now that we're on the mainland.

We were at lunch to come to a new understanding, nothing grand, I don't think, but between us, father and son, the child and the man. There were things he wanted to discuss, to get straight, out onto the table.

It's true I choked on the pan-seared whatnots. I remember everything was fine until I realized that I forgot to use my knife in an effort to eat more quickly than my father. I could feel the food getting lodged in my throat.

I could hear myself choking and others laughing.

Then I think my father called the waitress over and she got behind me to do the maneuver.

Then I think I was on the ground and all of them were taking turns kicking me and going through my pockets.

I looked at my father and said I expected better from you.

He apologized, said it wasn't personal.

I should probably say that I didn't know the man was planning to jump out of his hotel window, that he'd already composed a note.

Then I think I remember everyone screaming and yelling and others laughing and choking after he'd jumped off the balcony and made a mess of himself on the sidewalk.

I think maybe there were a lot of questions and I tried to provide answers.

The questions were about his mood, his business dealings, his personal life.

The answers always came down to your guess and mine.

They asked what it was like growing up and I told them he said we had to divvy up the woman's work because our mother decided everything was too much for her.

He said in the end all you have is the natural use of the woman. He said other than that everything is hopeless and too much to ask.

Otherwise we weren't permitted to talk about my mother, so God rest her soul if she is actually dead.

I do remember the day my father wanted to fish in the river but we didn't have poles or bait. He said that Jesus was a fisherman but that he fished people instead of fish. He said that's how great Jesus was, that he could fish people. He said we should go swimming instead since we didn't have poles. He said that Jesus walked on the water and it was a miracle.

He said that Jesus was an only son and love his only concept. Now strangers come in foreign tongues and dirty up the doorstep.

In this he meant South Americans and Europeans, I'm almost sure. He said they were all philistines and sodomites.

I watched him strip off his clothes and jump in. He kept on his shorts and told me to do likewise. He said God wanted us to be decent in front of each other.

I'd never been in a river before and no one ever told me about the currents. It was maybe two or three seconds before I started drowning. I was getting sucked under and pulled away and I swallowed a lot of water by the time my father saved me and dragged me to the shore. I think he had to pound on my chest so I could breathe again. This is when my father asked if I'd forgotten how to swim and I said I'm not sure I ever learned.

They asked me what this has to do with his suicide.

I said you tell me.

I didn't mention my brothers because they aren't worth mentioning, not a single one of them.

These were the brothers my mother never told me about, the ones my father had with other people.

I only associated with them when I was sent to live with my father periodically. My mother and father took turns disappearing and so I got bounced back and forth between them.

The police said they found a note but it wasn't in a language anyone could recognize or read, except for what was written on the envelope.

Gone Beautiful in perfect English, scripted like calligraphy.

They gave it to me after they were finished with him and their investigation. I keep it in a drawer somewhere, but I'm thinking about hanging it up on a wall.

The police took turns beating me with nightsticks while we discussed my father. I asked them why and they said keep talking, shitbird.

The language my father created is a sight to see. There are lines and symbols and figures and it goes on for pages and pages.

This is what I try to remember about him above all.

I try not to think about my father making us hold hands and sacrific-
ing ourselves at the table before dinner. He'd pray for us out loud, in
front of everyone.

He prayed that this brother would field a ground ball, that brother
would finally take his hands out of his pants, another would someday
adhere to the sense God gave him.

I've forgotten what he prayed for in my direction. I was always last
and by then I'd stopped listening.

By then I'd started on dinner because if I didn't there wouldn't be
anything left to eat. It's that way in every big family I imagine. If you
want anything you have to fight for it.

In the Dim Light of a New Day

I find almost everything hard to believe is what the man sitting next to me says to the woman sitting next to him. It doesn't matter what it is anymore, he doesn't believe it. He says he can't believe what's happened to the United States of America, that it's not what the founders intended. I know what he means because I have moths in my apartment and I can't believe it either. They are pantry moths so every time I open the pantry I have to kill at least two or three of them. It's been like this for weeks now and yesterday there were worms crawling along the walls and ceilings. Larvae is the technical word for them and I can't believe this either. This is why I am on my way to the store for a special poison that will kill the moths and their larvae all at once. But I know the man next to me wouldn't care about the moths even if I told him. You can tell he doesn't have moths or larvae in his apartment by the way he's dressed in a fancy suit and tie, but it turns out he and his wife have decided to renew hostilities anyway. He says he can't take it anymore and that Janet doesn't want to start a family. She says she can't bring a child into this world. I don't know who Janet is but I can't say I blame her. I couldn't bring a child into this world, either. It might be the reason Esperanza and I broke up. I think she desperately wanted my children and I couldn't do it. Last I heard she married someone from work, someone who harassed her sexually but before they changed all the rules. The woman who isn't Janet or Esperanza and is sitting next to the rich guy on the subway says, in the dim light of a new day I know what you mean and then she says, I'll have your baby and the man answers, you will? And then she says, it might be retarded, though, and then the both of them laugh for what seems like a full five minutes. I don't know what she means by the dim light because the lights aren't dim on the subway car but it was morning so she was right about that part. It doesn't matter because they're still laughing when my stop comes but I can't even crack a smile because nothing is funny when you have pantry moths in your kitchen, regardless of what the founders intended. On my way through the closing doors I turn around and say to the both of them you wouldn't believe what I can't take anymore and this is when I finally do laugh even though nothing about this is at all funny.

Gone Beautiful

Someone is at the door and asking for help. This is like when I walk down the street and see a sign in a store window that says, Help Wanted. I always want to go into the store and ask what kind of help they need, if it is urgent, if someone needs medical attention. I always assume someone has collapsed and is dying on the floor, someone who can't breathe and is in cardiac arrest, convulsing.

This happens to me sometimes. My chest hurts and my vision blurs and my mouth goes dry and then I'm down. Only sometimes do I get the shakes. People are sometimes careful to step around me when I get the shakes. Sometimes people are good this way.

I feel a kinship with people when they step around me. I never look them in the eye because I am usually convulsing and I can't keep my eyes open. If I could I would thank them.

Other times they kick me repeatedly and rifle through my pockets.

This is why I never go into stores that have a Help Wanted sign up in the window, because I don't want to see something like this. Maybe certain people want to see something like this but they are one of two things and I'm neither.

I have been locked in my room for however many days now. I'd been planning on this for months so I've been hoarding food and water and other supplies.

I decided I needed time to think things through and figure out where my life is headed.

I haven't been to the noontime meeting and shared with the group and I haven't been out on furlough, either.

How I pass the time is I read my books or I draw stick figures on the walls and floors.

I draw stick figures in relation to other stick figures. Some stick figures are standing in traffic while others rush over to beat them senseless or usher them to safety. Some are sexually harassing an attractive hostess in the back of a restaurant, while others are against the wall and brutalized by police officers.

In one drawing there is one stick figure driving a car and another in the passenger seat. In the next drawing the one in the passenger seat goes through the windshield and lands in a bloody heap some twenty feet away. Right next to that picture is a mother stick figure putting makeup on a child stick figure and then taking his photograph. This stick figure is looking up at his stick mother with an expression that is inscrutable.

Maybe the best one is a stick figure playing tennis while another stick figure is chained to a radiator, bound and gagged.

I haven't seen Watermelon Man in a long time, not at the noontime meetings or in the yard or recreation center but I'm certain he is still inside.

I do not think that is him at the door asking for help because I would recognize his voice.

It's possible that whoever is at the door and asking for help wants to come in because there is an active shooter in the building.

This would explain all the gunfire and screaming.

Hearing gunfire isn't unusual, but this amount of gunfire is.

There is a sign on my side of the door instructing us what to do in the event of fire, medical emergency, active shooter, hurricane, tornado, ice age, tsunami.

It's only during the active shooter scenario that you are supposed to locate and load all your guns and then hide under a bed or behind a chair with your favorite trained at the door.

Opening the door to someone asking for help is not on the list.

This is why I think this building used to be a high school because this sign couldn't pertain to us anymore. They confiscated all of our guns when they admitted us as guests that first day.

We haven't had an active shooter since I can't remember when, but that could be on account of my failing memory.

I also don't want to see if this isn't the case, if no one is on the floor and can't breathe, because then I'll want to know what the fuss is about. I'm not saying I want to see the senator on the ground like this, for instance, or the janitor who said what the fuck is a furlough, or Betty or Manny or even Trina or the other guests, but I don't think it would bother me. At least then someone would actually need help.

We are supposed to call each other guests. Not prisoners or detainees or hostages or captives. We are called guests because the state is housing us and we are trying to get better.

In one corner there is a stick figure eating pie after getting lost in a maze.

In another corner a stick figure is playing guitar and bleeding while singing Oye Como Va, mi ritmo, bueno pa' gozar, mulata.

Sometimes they march us into a room and have us perform tasks. This was before I locked myself in my room. I assume they still do this but I have no way of knowing.

They have other groups in other rooms that perform similar tasks and they compare the results. Then they shame one or both groups for their lackluster performance.

Today I remember my brother because he's probably dead and doesn't need help anymore.

The last time I saw my brother he needed all kinds of help. Machines were hooked into him for breathing and eating and using the restroom.

I tried depicting this in a drawing but I couldn't make the stick respirator look real. I also had trouble drawing a stick dialysis machine and stick catheter.

I keep a running tab of people who are probably dead and my brother and father are both on the list.

My father threw himself off the roof of a hotel one day after we had lunch some years ago. He'd left a note and said he'd gone beautiful, which was true. The note was in his very own language, which was likewise beautiful, like a cross between Arabic and Mayan hieroglyphs.

This I refuse to draw on the walls, though I'm sure it would be breathtaking. I can just imagine how I'd trace the stick figure plummeting through the air, graceful like a ballerina, and then crashing onto the pavement dead.

In my head he looks like the falling man from that photograph of the poor bastard who had to jump out of the towers as they burned.

But actually drawing this seems disrespectful.

I could never replicate the written language, either.

Tanya and my Sofia are probably both dead, too, along with the other brothers I sometimes lived with and couldn't stand the sight of.

I don't know how any of them died.

The gunfire is sporadic but steady. It sounds like a semiautomatic and like the shooter is going from room to room. This one sounds methodical, like he has an entire performance planned to the last detail. My guess is the shooter has several weapons, but I haven't heard anything like an explosion, so he probably doesn't have any grenades or IEDs.

I hear people running and screaming, though whenever there is gunfire the screaming is drowned out.

I assume the shooter is a man because most shooters are men and it seems that's all we have here.

It could be one of the guests but I'm guessing it's a staff member, either a supervisor or doctor or janitor.

I never need help when I'm out on furlough, but still people try to help me. They think I'm confused or trying to kill myself because I stand in traffic. They don't know that I'm out there trying to save the world.

They say that suicide runs in families but in this case I don't think it's true. Sometimes people usher me to the side of the road and beat me senseless. They tell me they do this for my own good. They tell me I shouldn't stand in traffic and ask me questions to find out if I'm South American or European.

I never tell them I'm half Rican.

It could be they only want help in the kitchen doing the dishes and that will be a disappointment. I don't like doing dishes and I don't think anyone can blame me. There is something wrong with my hands. I lose feeling. What happens is I start working with my hands and before long I feel the pins and needles and soon they go numb and I have to stop whatever it is I'm doing and shake them out.

I remember in the restaurant there was a Mexican named Roy-Boy who did the dishes and anything else I asked of him. He was a good one because he didn't harass Esperanza like his brother Jorge and the rest of the pendejos in the back.

No one knows what became of Roy-Boy but it's probably true that the police got him. If they found out he liked men during the interrogation then they probably beat him to death right then and there.

It is possible that the person at the door doesn't need help after all and the gunfire is the sound of the television in the rec room. It could be that it's a ruse because they think I have someone in here with me. We're not allowed to have overnight guests, especially if you have a history of chaining people to the radiator.

There is a pause in the gunfire, but not the screaming.

It could be the shooter needs a break or has to reload or perhaps he is on the phone with a negotiator. Perhaps they are trying to strike a deal so they can come in to treat the wounded.

I know I am safe inside my room and that it's probably not the shooter at the door asking for help.

If I still had a gun I would have it out and trained on the door.

Instead I am drawing a stick figure lying on the ground with kindred stick figures stepping around him as he convulses and writhes.

Notice how no one is kicking this stick figure or rifling through his pockets.

When people hear about this on the news I wonder if they will think I'm the shooter.

I think it's possible for some of them to think this, like maybe Django or Roy-Boy, but not Manny or Esperanza.

Not the people who know anything about me is what I'm saying.

I won't say more than this because who cares.

It's like when I was a kid and I would ask my mother for help with my homework. I can't remember what she said, but I'm sure it proves my point.

Acknowledgements

The author gratefully acknowledges the editors of the publications where these stories first appeared, some under different titles and in different forms.

"Furloughs" appeared in *Epiphany Magazine*
"The People Who Need It" appeared in *Pie & Whiskey*
"Even the Moonlight Is Blinding" appeared in *The Southampton Review*
"Roy-Boy" appeared in *The Collagist*
"Three Kinds of People" appeared in *Vice Magazine*
"The Sexual Ramifications of Coffee" appeared in *Willow Springs*
"Woodpecker Pie for Christmas" appeared in *The Inlander*
"How to Live, What to Do" appeared in *Caketrain*
"Which One's Will" appeared in *Apogee Journal*
"Decisions" appeared in *New World Writing*
"Eviction Notice" appeared in *People Holding*
"Bloodlines" appeared in *Sententia*
"The Natural Use of the Woman" appeared in *The Ampersand Review*
"Gone Beautiful" appeared in *Fence*
"A Good Percentage" appeared in *The Collagist*
"The Trouble with Paddling" appeared in *Hobart*

"The Dahlberg Repercussions" appeared in *New World Writing*

"Two Syndromes at Once" appeared in *Fanzine*

"To Grow Old in America" appeared in *Hunger Mountain*

"This Is Me After Dance Class" appeared in *New Flash Fiction Review*

"Buggery" appeared in *Hunger Mountain*

"A Better Class of People" appeared in *Hunger Mountain*

"The Future Home of the Wymans" appeared in *Big Other*

"What Is or Isn't Collapsing" appeared in *Okey Pankey*

"What The Living Emit" appeared in *Puerto Del Sol*

Special thanks to Michelle Dotter and Steve Gillis. Likewise special thanks to Jennifer Pommiss and Toni Lopez. Regular amount of thanks to Sam Ligon, Peter Markus, David McClendon, John Madera. Thanks to other people, too, the ones I've already thanked in previous books. You know who you are.